YARD WARS

YARD WARS

GLENN D. GLASGOW

Archway Publishing books may be ordered through booksellers or by contacting:

Archway Publishing
1663 Liberty Drive
Bloomington, IN 47403
www.archwaypublishing.com
844-669-3957

ISBN: 978-1-6657-5815-4 (sc)
ISBN: 978-1-6657-5817-8 (hc)
ISBN: 978-1-6657-5816-1 (e)

Library of Congress Control Number: 2024905469

Print information available on the last page.

Archway Publishing rev. date: 04/02/2024

Your eyes can absorb what your stomach can't stand. This was evident in the events across the street from Oscar's house where the Becks, one of the few families in the neighborhood, live. In regular times, the Beck family living inside the house at number 15 Chancellery Street includes the mom, Mrs. Beck, a retired English schoolteacher who spends most of her days now sewing, knitting, and cuddling on the couch with her tuxedo cat named Virgil. Also, the dad, Mr. Beck, is a retired firefighter who was with the fire department for over twenty years before retirement. Nowadays, he spends most of his time on his computer following and trying to outsmart the algorithms that dictate the stock market.

The Beck's only child is their daughter, Angela, a young lady in her mid to upper twenties. She sometimes lives with them but often spends her days on her college campus to be closer to her boyfriend, whom her parents have never met. Angela is an aspiring nursing student on every honor roll since starting school. This has made Angela the apple of her parents' eyes. Like her mom, Angela has hair that does not reach past her neck and barely covers the green and orange flame tattoo right above her cervical vertebrae.

Usually, in the late afternoon, around 16:00, neighborhood kids of all ages, including those on skateboards and bikes, can be seen playing in the streets. But on this particular day, there weren't any. There was hardly any traffic on the road all afternoon, but that changed with the sight of a white SUV and the sound of its screeching tires racing down the street. The driver slammed on the brakes just before they arrived in front of the Beck's house. Now, behind the SUV, one could hear the sounds of the paramedics getting louder as they were coming down Chancellery Street.

Just ahead of the paramedic, the white SUV, with the driver-side window rolled down, came to a screeching halt. The driver, a young lady who appeared to be in her upper twenties to early thirties, pulled up and parallel-parked just ahead on the north side of the street in front of the Beck's house. The paramedics immediately stopped and parked behind the white SUV with the back of their ambulance adjacent to the entrance walkway to the Beck's house.

Three very fit gentlemen, two of whom looked like they had just walked out of the gym at the college they graduated from last week, got out of the front seats. Two of the paramedics immediately rushed into the house. The third, a man who could pass for their father, ran to the back of the ambulance and opened the door to retrieve what looked to be a stretcher.

The young lady, apparently Angela, hurried out of the SUV without shoes, wearing a white T-shirt and khaki shorts. She left the driver's side door open, ran towards the house, and stopped running when she arrived at the top of the front steps. As she fumbled for the keys in front of the door, she dropped them, bent down, and quickly picked them up. She began to flip through her key ring, searching for the right key to unlock the front door for the two paramedics now standing next to her at the door. She found it, quickly opened the door, and bolted inside the house. Once inside the home, Angela and the paramedics were met in the living room by an elderly gentleman, Mr. Beck. He appeared to be in his mid to upper sixties, his hands trembling, blood on the palms of his hands, and on his face, a palm print from where he'd placed both of his hands on his cheeks.

Mr. Beck appeared confused and disoriented. Wearing a bathrobe and pajama pants in mismatched colors, he was sobbing as he stood in the living room, staring out the back window. When approached by Angela and the paramedics, he could only point toward the open door through the kitchen at the back of the house. Angela held him by the arm and walked him over to sit on the sofa. She then grabbed a few sheets of tissues from the tissue box on top of the nearby end table and began wiping off his face and hands.

The paramedics proceeded outside towards the back, where in the yard, they saw the man's wife, Mrs. Beck, who was now lying face down on her left side, with blood oozing from her nose. The drops of blood fell in a slow drip about seven seconds apart. Mrs. Beck also had scratch marks that now looked like open wounds covering her legs and arms, and what appeared to be burn marks were mixed in with dirt on several spots on her face, arms, and thighs. These parts of Mrs. Beck's body were exposed as she wore her favorite pink short-shorts and a white tank top, everyday attire to complement the beautiful and mild weather they had been experiencing lately. At first glance, the scratches on her body appeared to result from her scratching a rash that was spreading indiscriminately, or perhaps she'd had an allergic reaction to something she may have eaten or drank. If it was an allergy, its spread may indicate that the reaction had gotten out of control before she could obtain any allergy medicines, if any were available to her.

Lying on her back now and twisting her head from side to side slowly, she was barely breathing. Her eyes were wide open, and with her rapid mouth movement, she appeared to be gasping for air. She was trying to breathe and talk through her mouth simultaneously. There was not so much as a mumble. The soft blue blanket on which she lay on the ground was now covered partially with spots of blood and the droppings from the pieces of food she was eating. The half-eaten peanut butter and jelly sandwich on whole wheat bread, the empty twenty-ounce bottle of pineapple juice, and the palm-size chocolate chip cookie were scattered not just on the blanket but also on her clothes, with a few crumbs entangled in her hair, which seemed to indicate that she had food in her hand while she was scratching her head.

Angela now approached outside and, seeing her mom in this condition, fell to her knees and covered her mouth as she started to cry and scream, "NOOO…" Angela had to be partly restrained by one of the paramedics since when she bent over, she landed hands down and on her knees. She almost fell over as she tried to grab her mom by the arm.

Mr. Beck also came outside following Angela and instantly knelt beside his daughter, wrapping one of his arms around her and the other around Mrs. Beck. In doing so, he was leaving blood stains on the shoulder of Angela's clothes.

One of the paramedics turned to Angela, and Mr. Beck asked if they knew if she had a medical history of allergies, seizures, or any other medical conditions that may have caused her to appear as if she had passed out and was now struggling to stay awake. Mr. Beck and Angela raised their heads, looking to the paramedics to say no. Still sobbing, Mr. Beck said he was unaware of such a condition. What appeared to the paramedics at first glance to be some allergic reaction they now thought was much more severe.

The third paramedic, rolling a stretcher, now joined them outside. One of the first paramedics held Angela and her father's hands and raised them upright to move them out of the way so the other paramedics could lower the stretcher down to the ground next to Mrs. Beck. All three paramedics looked at each other, puzzled, wondering what the cause of this situation with Mrs. Beck could be. One of the paramedics got down on his knees next to Mrs. Beck and, with two fingers feeling her neck, tried to find a pulse to measure. He then grabbed her right hand at the wrist while holding his other hand still on the side of her neck, slightly below the jawbone, which, along with her neck, was now severely swollen. Although seemingly unrelated, while looking at the sweat on Mrs. Beck's face and neck, the paramedics asked Mr. Beck if he knew whether she was wearing any sunscreen, to which he answered, "I don't know."

As the paramedics looked around Mrs. Beck and the blanket, they saw the food droppings around her and nearby. Now, one of the paramedics asked Mr. Beck if perhaps Mrs. Beck had any food allergies that he was aware of, to which Mr. Beck replied no with two left-to-right shakes of his head.

He paused and added, "Not to my knowledge. As for the things she was eating, we both ate them regularly, and none of them has an expiration date," said Mr. Beck.

Angela continued her uncontrollable crying and held her mom's hand as her mom was now hoisted up by the underarms and legs and placed onto the stretcher. She barely opened her eyes and lips, and her mouth movements were now minimal, with her breathing reflecting the same. When the paramedics picked her up and placed her on the stretcher, she was facing straight up. The moment they let go of her, her head tilted back down to one side, and the bleeding from her nose continued. The paramedics then raised the stretcher and began to roll her out of the yard through the house and towards their waiting ambulance.

Still bent down, and through her tears, Angela and her father embraced each other. They then stood up and held each other around their waists as they balanced on each other. They continued through the house and outside together and got into the ambulance with Mrs. Beck.

Mrs. Beck was now in the back of the ambulance, her breathing more difficult than before, as the paramedics gave her oxygen. One of them placed a mask over her face while the other, holding a small flashlight, held it up to her face, held up his index finger, and asked her to open her eyes and follow his finger as he was trying to get a good look into the back of her eyes.

Angela and her father sat opposite Mrs. Beck in the ambulance, each holding one of her hands as the paramedics closed the back door and the driver took off, sirens blasting. On the way to the hospital, both paramedics in the back tried again to perform CPR. The two of them alternated, thumping her chest. Her breathing continued to decrease, so the CPR became more aggressive at a frantic pace. Angela and her dad sat there, sobbing and just watching. Seeing that the CPR wasn't working, one of the paramedics then turned and reached for the defibrillator.

Angela's crying continued, now even more pronounced, and the outbursts more frequent. Perhaps now, hearing his daughter's sobs made Mr. Beck's fear the worse, and his cries became louder, too.

"We're losing her! We're losing her!" Shouted one of the paramedics while looking at his handheld computer and heart monitor.

"We still have SIX minutes to get to the hospital," said the driver, looking back and talking over his shoulder, still speeding on their way.

The paramedics used the defibrillator two more times. Still, after the third attempt with the defibrillator, the sudden constant beeping sound from the pulse monitor machine went flat.

Inside, the ambulance grew silent. This silence included Angela and her dad, and their eyes were wide open as they suddenly stopped crying. Silence filled the space; the only sound anyone could hear was that of the engine and the sirens.

With her hands open, palms facing up, Angela asked, "What is happening?"

One of the paramedics turned to her, patted her on the shoulder, and said, "Calm down, Miss Angela, we're almost there."

About two minutes later, the ambulance arrived at the hospital. They were met by four other hospital staff members waiting outside the emergency entrance. The paramedics instantly received help, from opening the ambulance door to getting Mrs. Beck out and assisting in wheeling Mrs. Beck into the hospital. As Angela and her father jumped out and walked behind the hospital staff and Mrs. Beck, the driver shouted and waved to them, "Take care; I'll see you later."

Once through the entrance door, Mrs. Beck was rushed to the emergency operating room, where a doctor and additional staff awaited her. The hospital staff were rolling Mrs. Beck into the hospital so fast that only the staff and Angela could keep up with them. Mr. Beck shuffled after them, still wearing his bedroom slippers. He had both his hands on his hips and a wary look. He complained of being out of breath and that both his feet were in pain. He could not run or walk as quickly as the others, but the hallway was long enough to see where they were going. He could always approach one of the information desks and inquire where his wife would be placed if he got lost.

When the hospital staff and Angela reached a certain point, she was halted by a staff member. She was then told that she could not go beyond this point. The staff member told Angela that she and her father, who was still lagging, were not allowed to enter the room with her mom. They were then instructed to proceed to the family waiting room and remain there for the doctor to come out and contact them so he could give them further detailed information regarding her condition.

Once Mr. Beck arrived, Angela and her father waited for a few minutes, which seemed an eternity. There were some old magazines on the little table, dating back ten years, and the three televisions hanging on the wall offered them the choices of home remodeling, gardening, or cooking. Angela and her father made up one of three families waiting in that room. By now, both father and daughter had stopped crying, but they were still visibly shaken, their eyes bloodshot. Whatever eye makeup Angela was wearing now looked more like a Halloween facemask. Angela and her father sat on the waiting room bench, holding each other's hands with Angela's head on her father's shoulder and his head on hers.

About thirty minutes later, Dr. Morell came out, accompanied by another physician, Dr. Bloch. They did not make eye contact with Angela and her father, and neither of the doctors smiled as they walked toward them. Angela and her father stood up. The primary physician, Dr. Morell, turned to Mr. Beck and Angela; he held out his hands, grabbed one of Mr. Beck's and Angela's hands, and said softly while shaking his head, "I'm so sorry, but she did not make it."

Angela dropped to her knees, raised her still partially blood-stained hands in the air, and with her eyes closed, she screamed out with a loud and long, "NOOOOOO!"

As Dr. Morell held her father's hand, Mr. Beck's hands and knees, his entire body began to shake. Dr. Morell slowly sat him back down on the waiting room bench. The second doctor, Dr. Bloch, looked over to Angela, still on the floor. Dr. Bolch held Angela's arm and helped her to get back up to her feet. After Mr. Beck was placed back on the bench. Dr. Bloch walked Angela back over to sit down next to her father. Both doctors now put one hand around Mr. Beck's and the other doctor's hand around Angela's shoulders to comfort them. Dr. Bloch added, "We did all we could."

In a whispering conversation with Mr. Beck, Dr. Bloch wanted to know where Mrs. Beck was when she received those scratches all over her body. Scratches that resulted in not just severe swelling but also bleeding. Dr. Morell said that the bleeding that was coming through her mouth and nose proved to be the result of something else more serious. "I have ruled out some severe infections, but it will need further investigation," he said.

Dr. Morell went on to say that the scratches on Mrs. Beck looked almost like burn marks, and they were odd because they covered so many areas of her body but were not in her hair. Dr. Morell also said he believed that the severe swelling was what led to her breathing problem. The swelling squeezed the airways, restricting airflow, and contributed to this situation. Both doctors stood before Mr. Beck and Angela, explaining their thoughts, and Mr. Beck and Angela sat still with tears in their eyes, listening without interruption. Dr. Morell went on to say that there was no way to know for sure without an autopsy. Dr. Bloch then informed Mr. Beck that an autopsy would be conducted in the next few days. This would enable the entire team to come to a definite conclusion about what caused this incident.

Mr. Beck, with his speech blurred and pausing between each of his words, told the doctor that all he could recall was that she was sitting outside, catching some sun, and enjoying a few snacks in the backyard. He related that at one point, she had some music playing from the cassette of her summer favorite recordings that she had for over twenty years. Then abruptly, at one point, the music stopped when she brought the portable stereo inside, and this was when she came in to get one of the small bottles of pineapple juice out of the fridge. When she stood up, though, she was using a towel and was dusting off her body, which he assumed was just dirt from the yard. Mr. Beck said he thought his wife was enjoying a solo picnic when she went back outside, then, a few minutes later, he suddenly heard her screams. He went out and saw that she was scratching frantically. At that point, she was bleeding. He asked her what was wrong, but she did not answer; she just kept rubbing.

At this point, he said he panicked, and the first person he called was Angela. While on the phone, he said Angela, who was in her dorm with her boyfriend then, told him not to worry and that she would call 911. Angela, sitting next to Mr. Beck, nodded her head in agreement. At this point, Dr. Bloch interrupted Mr. Beck and advised him and Angela to go home and get some rest, as there was nothing else they could do while waiting around at the hospital, and both doctors began to leave. Both the doctors, Morell and Bloch, left the waiting room area. However, about two hours later, Angela and her father were still sitting at the hospital, waiting for other relatives to show up. In those several hours, though, only one relative showed up. He was Angela's uncle, her father's brother, and he came riding on a motorcycle.

Dr. Morell later returned to the waiting room, where he again encountered Angela, Mr. Beck, and the uncle, and explained to them that there was nothing they, referring to first the paramedics and then the hospital staff here, could have done differently that could have saved Mrs. Beck's life. He said that on her way to the hospital, she was already gone, and all attempts to revive her had failed. He offered his condolences and advised them that all three needed to go home to make final arrangements, including notifying all the other concerned family members. All three nodded in agreement.

Understanding that the uncle came riding on a motorcycle while Angela and her father were still waiting for a ride since they arrived via the ambulance, Dr. Morell asked Mr. Beck and Angela if they needed a ride home. Mr. Beck nodded, saying yes; they were still waiting, so Dr. Morel did not want them to wait any longer. He instructed the hospital staff to provide a ride service to take them back to their house.

*T*oday is 07-07, James Bond Day. On this day, Oscar Abhor, the neighbor who lived in the house directly across the street from the Beck family, would, for the longest time, refer to it as "Double O seven day."

There remains some disagreement, though, among the diehard fan club members and Oscar as to when this holiday officially started. Some, though, primarily diehard fans, would always consider James Bond Day as the day the first movie was released back in 1961. But not Oscar; for him, it would always be July 7, or 07 07, as he puts it.

While most of Oscar's buddies and other guys in the neighborhood would be watching a sporting event or something similar on any given Saturday or even Sunday, those events were not always for Oscar to celebrate, at least not on Double O seven days.

Being the stubborn man he is, on James Bond Day, or Double O seven-day as he always called it, he believed everyone should at least follow his lead and call the day for what, in his world, he truly believed it represented.

On James Bond Day, unlike any other weekend day, Oscar would place himself in front of his TV with the remote in one hand and a beer in the other. He'd place a second beer on the end table for later. When this second beer is at room temperature, for Oscar, that is when beer tastes best. He would be most comfortable with his legs crossed and his feet propped up atop the ottoman. Oscar would only have to move to get something else to eat or drink, and the only other interruption would be his wife Penni asking him a question or his having to get up to use the bathroom. If he could get away with it, he would like to binge-watch every 007 movie his heart could manage and have Penni bring all his meals to him, provided he could do all this without falling asleep.

When Oscar was younger, he saw his first James Bond film, *Dr. No.* He was mesmerized by his father and older brother, and he wanted to see that film repeatedly, as he became addicted. When it came out, he saw this movie in the cinema and was in his final year of high school. The film had been on Oscar, his brother, and his father's timetable ever since it was advertised as scheduled to be released. Still, they had not had the chance to see it together until that day when their schedules finally aligned after waiting for more than a week. Oscar's mother never shared the same enthusiasm as his father and brother. She loved the cinema, but the films about romance and comedies were her favorites.

Today, Oscar is a grown adult, standing a little over 192cm, not overly tall, and weighing just shy of 100kg. With his bleached blond receding hairline, the gray hair was now not as prominent as it was years gone by, but at least he could still comb the ones in the back of his head. He rose noticeably, standing beside his family members or in a crowd.

Excessive exposure to the sun was most noticeable on his neck and upper back; this was where the 24-karat gold rope necklace he got from his parents when graduating from high school used to hang. Now, though, it looked more like a scar he got in his wilder days when he was a younger man at his first job as a lifeguard. The scar snaked around and through the fluorescent spots around his neck.

To make matters worse, Oscar tended to go about in and around the house without wearing any shirt, especially when doing his yard work and most chores, such as washing the car. Oscar had done this so often that he dressed like this during the non-warm months. Oscar's typical attire consisted of light-colored shorts and jeans. He mostly wore flip-flops, and at other times, he'd go barefoot.

One could consider him as being "hip" for an older gentleman. His choice of limited clothing could easily be classified as up-to-date. He would dress up when he had to put on a more professional or semi-professional outfit for places such as the doctor's office, HOA meetings, or excellent restaurants. Still, he often wore khaki shorts and a polo shirt.

Doing hard work was what he considered one of— if not the *only* form of extreme exercise he got. His other regular exercise consisted of performing essential repairs in and around the house and occasionally doing the dishes. Judging by his physical appearance, most would think Oscar was the type of person who could say whatever was on his mind without fear of reprisals, and in doing so, he would encounter little if any resistance to his opinion, and they would be correct. He sometimes argued about every subject and raised his voice to get the point across.

On James Bond Day, Oscar always takes some time, with his wife's blessing, away from whatever he considers one of his normal weekend activities. He enjoys those weekends when the grandkids come over, and he gets to play games with them and take them shopping or to a matinee. But Double O Seven days were Oscar's time to be unproductive and lazy. Being productive typically included doing what he wanted or didn't mind helping with, not necessarily what his wife's nagging compelled him to do. These activities could consist of a round of golf with his friends, reading either the newspaper or a sports or mechanic-type magazine, and, of course, doing some gardening—Well, to be fair, yard work.

Yes, today is 007 day, and for Oscar, it is a day made for relaxing, which means spending some of it alone in front of the TV, processing his thoughts and contemplating his life. When reflecting on his life, he liked to think he had no regrets. Oscar would do this mostly while he sat in front of the tube to either watch any one of the James Bond movies he had in his existing collection or while armed with the remote and flipping through the channels, where he could always come across a Bond movie marathon playing on one of the many commercial channels.

Oscar had yet to fall in love with streaming on the TV, computer, or phone for any of his on-demand movies. These were not necessarily the shows or movies he wanted to see at any given moment. And if a Bond movie were not playing on one of the many commercially available channels, he would rather watch one from his collection.

During channel surfing, of course, he was likely to find a Bond film somewhere. Even if he caught one that was already in progress, even if that movie is more than halfway through, it is still worth watching for Oscar. To him, finding something almost over doesn't mean he will rewind it from the start. No, to him, this means that somewhere out there, someone else is celebrating James Bond Day right along with him, so now it is as if he is watching it with a long-lost friend.

Please don't say he is old or old-fashioned; he prefers nostalgia. Oscar would describe his taste and style as having a greater appreciation for how things used to be in the past. This was especially evident regarding some of the old technologies he liked to use.

Oscar could still choose between the VHS or Laserdisc versions of the movies from his collection, and yes, he had both players. He also had a few of the films in his collection that were duplicated in both formats. Oscar does not like to play favorites when it comes to his technology, but sadly, even worse for Oscar, the most recent Bond films are now only available on DVD, Digital Blu-ray, and streaming, so for this reason, Oscar has not stooped to that level of purchase or agreed to have his technology upgraded.

Oscar did not want to hear about how good the picture quality was, or especially anything about what he referred to as "The New Whipper Snappers," these being the new actors that lately played the part of Bond.

Although they have become more popular, they're still not for him and never will be. That's not to say he can't watch one of their movies, but there's no love lost between him and the newer Bonds. His favorite actor to play the role in any of the films remains Sir Roger Moore (14th October 1927-23rd May 2017), followed by his second favorite, Sir Sean Connery (25th August 1930- 31st October 2020).

In any rare conversation with friends or family where such a discussion would involve any of the Bond movies, Oscar could readily point out most, if not all, the flaws. These flaws ranged from not just filming locations but also in dialogue. His all-time favorite flaws to highlight were the on-location scenes. That is when the movie has an outdoor walking, running, or a car chase scene. Here, the car chase goes up and then comes down any street in, say, London. This is where Oscar would point out, "You see that? The cars will then take a right or left turn at any one corner, and then suddenly, they are in a different part of the city." To any otherwise unsuspecting person unfamiliar with the scenery or layout of London and its neighborhoods, there would be no problem, and they would not have noticed the difference. Still, for Oscar, this was a major pet peeve.

He would argue that the street the car turned onto, from where it had just come from, was too far from the other street. When something like that happened, whether or not he had an audience to speak to, Oscar would raise his hands and clasp them on his head, saying aloud, "You see, they think we're stupid." He would usually say this to his wife, Penni, or whoever else was there, and it would make no difference to him whether or not that person was listening. He would say, "Those two streets are in no way that close to each other."

His wife, Penni, would sometimes smile and nod. Penni would do this, not in agreement, but to acknowledge that she has heard it all before, even though Oscar may or may not know whether he had pointed this or that scene out once or twice. If he did, perhaps it was in a whisper or at least a passing comment. He could not resist. He would point out these errors without hesitation while praising every other moment of the film, especially the stunts. As he puts it, the stunts in the different parts of the movies that feature one of his "good ole boys," code words meaning Roger Moore and Sean Connery—these stunts he liked, where the "newbie whipper-snappers" do not appear.

A View to a Kill with Roger Moore had always been his favorite go-to Bond flick, though, and that was not because he thought it had the best script or acting. Oh no, that was because it contained scenes of his favorite cities, Paris and San Francisco. The scenes that were shot in those two cities, when seen on the big screen, would give him pause, and seeing parts of those cities would give him a reason to reminisce about times past, times to reflect on and romanticize the experiences he had when he was visiting each city, years ago, as a student.

Oscar once said he thought both cities were the same, not only for their collective love of art or uniquely grand architecture but also for their liberal lifestyle and tendencies to attract a younger, more affluent, well-educated, and open-minded group of individuals. These were individuals who not only wanted to live there but also wanted to visit multiple times. With a beer in one hand and the banana in the other, he was ready to start his day or at least continue his distinctive holiday tradition.

Oscar's better half was Penelope, Penni, for short, and she spelled it slightly differently with an 'I' and not a 'y' at the end. There was this one occasion when Penni sat down and watched a Bond film with him, and that film became her favorite. It was the first and only one she'd ever seen with him, *On Her Majesty's Secret Service*. Penni's reasoning for liking that film, as she later stated, was she loved the idea of the essential theme that a man with a *License to Kill* will do anything in order to do so, not for God, but for the queen and country.

They had met many years before while both were on vacation as students. He was traveling solo, and she was with her older sister, a sister who passed away almost one year before, a day that Penni has always remembered vividly.

The day Penni's sister died was not an out-of-the-ordinary weekend day. Like Mrs. Beck, coincidentally enough, she was also lying out under the sun. But unlike Mrs. Beck, Penni's sister was fully clothed, complete with sunscreen covering all the exposed parts of her body that her clothes did not hide. She also had a hat that provided shade over her face and down her neck. A physician conducted a later autopsy and concluded that without releasing specific details as to the particular cause of why her body went into shock, the autopsy determined that she died as a result of cardiac arrest.

The autopsy stated that this occurred after her blood pressure suddenly dropped dangerously low, and her airways narrowed, which then first restricted and ultimately prohibited her breathing. The sudden drop sent her heart rate racing but with a feeble pulse. When Penni discovered her sister's condition and saw that she had passed, there was vomit on her sister's clothing and a rash on the side of her stomach and right arm. Penni seldom liked to talk about her sister's passing. It was a subject that caused her headaches and grief. At those times, she would return to Oscar to reminisce about happier times that involved just Oscar and herself.

The time of Oscar and Penni's first meeting occurred while both were on a Scandinavian vacation cruise. It was a chance encounter once the ship was docked in Helsinki Harbor. One night at a concert aboard the cruise ship, with Penni's sister sitting next to her on one side, Oscar and Penni just happened to have seats next to each other on the other side. After a brief introduction by Penni's sister, a conversation between Oscar and Penni soon followed. This conversation lasted for several hours, even after the concert had ended and everyone else on the ship had either returned to their cabins or one of the many bars and clubs on board the vessel.

After that night, the rest of Penni's and Oscar's encounters became history. When Oscar and Penni sit on the couch, they sometimes reminisce about that chance encounter and discuss the what-ifs. *What if* they had never booked that trip? *What if* Penni's sister had never introduced them, and *what if* they had never had seats next to each other?

Married now for over thirty-five years, these days, most of their conversations were more about the present day and the future; they seldom centered around their son. Penni rarely got on Oscar's case about most of the petty things, especially those things needing to get done in and around the house. Recently, however, more so in the past few days, a pet peeve of hers has been the volume of leaves accumulating not just in their yard but also in their neighbor's yard.

Although most people would consider the neighbor's yard none of their business, Penni, and to a lesser degree Oscar, made it their business, at least in discussions between themselves.

With the next HOA meeting scheduled in less than a week, rest assured that the issue of the leaves blowing all over the neighborhood streets will be on the agenda for Oscar's wife, Penni. Penni certainly anticipated that some neighbors, particularly the Becks and Mr. Mark, who have been vocal in the past, would be less receptive to the feeling or idea that they are being told what to do or how they should keep their most significant investment presentable. The neighbors would likely not take it well to be told they must have the same standards of liking and cleanliness as someone else. With the recent passing of Mrs. Beck, Mr. Beck, and Angela would not have the patience or interest to listen to criticism about their family. To at least the neighbors like the Becks and the Marks, Penni was their Karen.

Oscar had his eyes on the houses to his immediate left and right. On more than one occasion, he did mention to Penni that he often wished he could own all the houses on his block and in this neighborhood. Oscar explained to Penni that his rationale was that he could have just his and her family occupying the entire block and neighborhood. He would say this by stressing that their families, especially the kids, could play in their streets among their "own kind," as he put it. Oscar said this situation would happen without the roar of outsiders' cars cruising or racing up and down their street. As an added perk, with just their families occupying the entire neighborhood, the neighborhood would be on the watch if anyone outside were ever tempted to break into one of the homes to commit any crime. That's also because he would ensure everyone had keys to everyone else's house, making it easy for them to respond to cries for help. If such a thing were to happen, once confronted, that criminal would have nowhere within the community to run and hide. Plus, as a bonus, when the kids were out playing, and it started to grow dark, they could have dinner and even have sleepovers in whatever house the dusk or a heavy downpour found them in without the parents having to worry about where the kids were at a particular time of the night.

Since Oscar and Penni were both now retired, on most of their lazy days, Penni would let him enjoy occasional TV binge-watching, particularly his occasional must-see sports. Oscar would do the same for her when it was her turn for something she must see on the tube, but usually, that was rare.

For Penni, though, her TV interests were most often celebrity reality shows, especially those shows where they have to select from a bunch of people in different situations to try and find a mate from several other contenders, and the show where celebrities have their dance off contests, you know the ones where the contestants are eliminated one by one each week.

When it comes to sports, Penni enjoyed anything involving athletics. Triathlons and marathons mostly got her undivided attention. Oscar did share some of her enthusiasm, at least in athletics. So, whenever any competitions were on TV, they could sit and watch them together. They each had their favorites, but usually, they'd be rooting for the same team or contestants.

Oscar once said, "Athletes are superior to all other humankind, especially those with my body frame, built just like me and our extended family." Oscar once said that the ones who look like him and act just like him are the ones who display tremendous endurance, strength, and power. He said that, as a society, his people had this special gift to achieve whatever they wanted. "Once we have this," he added, "we can gracefully accomplish much."

Usually, Penni would smile at him when he made these comments, and she would do that without sometimes staring or looking directly at him. She would continue whatever activity she was involved in without commenting on what was just said.

Compared to their neighbors' yards, granted the concern was only for the leaves piling up, Oscar and Penni Abhor's yard could easily pass as decorative and colorful art. Never one to be silent, Oscar Abhor did intend to bring up the leaf situation again at the upcoming HOA meeting, just as he did last season.

The last time the yard situation was mentioned, the Beck household vocally challenged any suggestions that they, or anyone else, should be subjected to listening to criticism from another homeowner about their home, let alone their yard. But Mrs. Beck, may she forever rest in peace, is no longer around. The last time the situation with the yard was mentioned, Mr. Beck even went so far as to stand up, walk over, and, while directly facing Oscar, say that as neighbors, they have no right to judge without—at the very least—first having a tour and taking a good look at their property.

This time around, though, Oscar was armed with pictures he had taken with his camera over the last few days and weeks. He was confident he could convince the entire HOA, or at least most of the members on the board, to see this point of view and bring about a vote on an ultimatum, saying if the homeowners don't clean up their yards by a specific due date, the HOA could begin foreclosure proceedings on their property. This would be music to Oscar's ears, as he could buy the property in foreclosure.

Oscar said he was willing to bypass the usual warnings in the form of flyers and letters dispatched to each homeowner and go straight to this more drastic measure since this situation with the yard happens every season.

Penni was very meticulous when it came to her home and gardening efforts. In addition to that, particular attention was always paid to the cleanliness of the inside of her house. But just like every home, no matter the level of care and cleanliness, these homes always had a few of what Oscar often called "vermin." These "vermin," Oscar once said, will somehow always find a way to get into his home and every home within the community. He feared that if left unattended, these vermin would eventually take over and destroy his family's home and everything they had worked so hard to accomplish all these years. After all, these vermin were witty and clever at avoiding detection until it was too late. All these leaves scattered over the yard offered these vermin protection, a place to hide, grow, and spread while avoiding detection.

Recently, Oscar had noticed that they had also become very resistant to almost every other toxic maneuver he had used on them. While laughing, he once commented to Penni that he had even seen them drinking the pesticide he used on them and that he would need a new, routine solution and a more aggressive plan to rid his house and yard of these vermin once and for all.

The path that Liz could be seen strolling along this misty morning was the same route she always took to get fresh water for her entire family, but only when the responsibility was her turn. As of late, and since she was the only daughter and the middle child, it was a responsibility she did not equally share with her two brothers. Unfortunately for Liz, they—as of late—were always busy elsewhere, doing boy stuff, so often that the water-gathering responsibility fell to her without fuss or debate from Liz.

With her lean athletic build, Liz did not display too much muscle, just a more toned yet well-defined physique. She could make any task designated for a man with brains and brawn look simple. In conversations with her, one never had to repeat directions or procedures. She could assemble the most complicated project without reading the directions or get from point A to point B without reading the map.

Sometimes, for her siblings and family to communicate with her, they only had to look at her, wave, or make eye movements, and she would completely understand what they were trying to convey. She could, at times, with a smile or wink, finish their sentences, thus leaving them with the feeling of déjà vu. Whenever there were questions about something or someone needed help with something, Liz was one of the most sought-after volunteers.

To the unfamiliar eye, the path would appear covered with black ice, very well polished, and slippery most of the way. But that could be because it was partially covered with some light brown and green algae-looking particles, resulting from dead leaves accumulated over the season, primarily on the corners where the concrete slabs would meet the grass along the walkway in the front of Oscar's yard. Maybe it was the water from the recent morning show, where the devil and his wife fought, with no clear winner declared. Or it could also have been that the leaves dried up so much that they were at the point of no-return decomposition, and these leaves had now created their soil. That soil lay just beneath the slow, smooth water flow, including water excreted from the sprinkler system or the runoff from the recent rain of the past week. At best, those would be well-educated guesses. Still, Liz assumed this water resulted from the constant dripping, courtesy of Oscar and his wife's outdoor water hose.

The water always forked through first between the spacing of the slabs and where the concrete pieces barely met. This was where, whenever the cracks were filled, all the small creatures avoided passing inside these cracks. From this point, the water flowed uninterrupted towards the street, eventually into the sidewalk, and down the drain.

Nothing in these cracks could escape the water's destructive role during unexpected heavy rains. This would include the ants who would otherwise be considered safe in their mounds, depending on how well they were constructed. Some of these mounds could be regarded as architectural masterpieces the ants had made into their home. Unfortunately, these masterpieces were placed in the water's direct path. Still, this path was always considered prime real estate for its proximity and access to all that fresh water.

Aside from the rain and the dripping water hose, each time Oscar and Penni had their water hose turned on to water their grass or the lawn, some—not all—the sand from the foundation of the various mounds would get washed away. However, some structural outlines, such as the foundation, would remain intact when this happened. After the rain or heavy water flow, all the ants, regardless of age or sex, would soon be seen carrying a few grains of sand at a time as they worked to rebuild what had just washed away.

When it came time to rebuild the mounds, the ants would follow each other in a particular path due to their pheromones, which gave off a chemical smell excreted through their bodies, and that scent kept all the other ants in line. This same phenomenon was repeated when transporting and stocking up on food.

Every time the water flow was turned on by either the sprinklers or rain, it was always a cause for concern that some ants would be exposed to the open world. This would be an invitation for predators, particularly the lizards, who often seize an opportunity for an easy and defenseless meal. Since the lizards can live in any environment except for extreme freezes or the oceans, this location within the grounds of Oscar's yard was ideal.

However, due to their vast numbers, ants could easily outnumber and overwhelm a wounded lizard, and an injured lizard was not so much a usual sight or occasion. Suppose there was such a site where a wounded lizard was dying that would provide meals for the ants for a long time. But not for all the ants, as some respected and admired various lizards. As an added fun fact, the ants knew very well that the total weight of all the ants on earth was roughly equal to that of all the humans on earth; yes, their vast numbers gave them confidence.

When planning for emergencies, just like on our road signs, the ones that warn and advise about evacuation routes and procedures to follow for natural disasters such as hurricanes, tornadoes, and floods, there were substantial warnings posted throughout and around the various mounds. These warnings were about what to do based on the perceived threat, whether that threat was from nature or a predator. These were warnings of the dangers of encountering not just the water and lizards but also some of the other creatures, such as snails, beetles, caterpillars, and frogs, all of them lurked around, just outside the safety provided by the walls of the mound.

This day was not much different from previous days, as it was not uncommon for Liz to be alone or walk up this particular path that she knew so well. This path went straight, just past the giant mound.

Looking on from the sidelines with caution, the ants would always be on the lookout, spying on everything passing by. The ants particularly suspicious of the lizards were those unfamiliar with Liz or who had never interacted with her or every other lizard across the yard. Those unfamiliar with Liz would think she, just like their regular ant spies, was out and about looking for food or could pass by to gather information about the ants to report to the other lizards.

Occasionally, a few ants would peek out and see Liz passing by. However, as soon as Liz stopped and turned around and did not necessarily look at them, they would still duck back down and hide just below the surface to be ready to alert the other ants—should the need arise—if what they thought was imminent danger lay ahead.

The sun's rays had yet to overcome the mist fully, but it was noticeably brighter now than earlier. This was alright for the ants on an otherwise uneventful morning. Shade for the ant spies was provided by some of the bent-in-the-middle brown maple leaves lying on the ground and the branches from the trees above that stretched over the yard and across the road.

From the branches of the trees above, where both ants and lizards would sometimes compete for food and storage, the air was not yet filled with the smell of the various kitchens in the neighborhood making their breakfast. This morning, like others, was also about the usual smell from the cars with engines running and badly needing an oil change, getting ready to take their owners to work.

Some of the leaves from Oscar's yard had accumulated neatly into a dense pile, now standing about four feet tall. The rest of the leaves had gathered together and formed a colorful carpet, blanketing most of his yard here and there with single leaves. In contrast, some other leaves covered most of everyone's yard, the road, and the neighborhood. However, when viewed from this high up above, in the trees, the leaves created an abstract piece of artwork or a puzzle that looked like it was either missing its corners or was left deliberately unfinished by the artists.

Besides the Beck's home, across the street was one of the other houses that Oscar hoped to be able to buy soon, the Mark's house. The Kyrie family, a family of Red Harvester ants, lived in Mr. Mark's yard. They were the largest tribe of ants in this neighborhood, and their numbers could easily be in the hundreds of thousands. No one had considered counting, but when they got together, moving large objects like maple leaves or skeletons, one could quickly determine that their numbers were substantial. They were led by their queen, Valerie, Queen V for short. Queen V was older than most queens and had served longer than any other queen in recent memory. She has witnessed some of history's most bloody and dire battles. She was well-loved among the fire ants as her words of wisdom had always inspired them throughout the most challenging times.

Although Queen V was extremely popular throughout her reign, according to the polls, as of late, she has fallen behind in the hearts and minds of many ants who felt she had gotten too soft on those who threatened them. Some of those critics have accused her of not being aggressive enough in protecting the various mounds and colonies from outside threats; her lack of a robust plan has allowed outsiders to take advantage of this weakness. It is a subject that she was concerned her opponents would make a central theme in a future election.

In the ant world, over 12,000 individual species of ants exist. Compared to other ants, there aren't many visible distinctions among the particular ant species or colonies. However, if you were bitten by one of these fire ants, you would know the difference as you would be in for a lot of pain. The queen ants do have wings, which she will eliminate every time she needs to start a new nest. The conditions for creating a new nest were mainly determined by nature and usually a representation of either the destruction of the old mound or the election of a new queen, usually upon the death of the current queen. Once mated, the queen will not leave the nest again. Once she dies, the colony dies.

However, various kinds of ant colonies survived throughout this neighborhood. Depending on the group, a single colony could contain millions of ants. But these various colonies had three basics: a queen, female, and male. Males serve no purpose beyond mating, after which they will die . In addition, the queen also had her set of soldiers whose sole job was to defend the colony with their lives and protect the queen at all costs.

Most of these ants' lifespans seldom exceeded a few months at best, except for some queen ants, who lived for many more years. This also means they could have millions of babies. Unfortunately for the ants, if by chance their queen dies, that colony was likely only to survive a few more months at most. The queens are seldom replaced; without the queen, the other ants in the colony would find it nearly impossible to reproduce.

Like Liz in her lizard family, most of the ant jobs in the colony were done by female ants. All of the ant workers in the colony had individual jobs. When it came to jobs for the ants, in addition to the building of the colony, the ant jobs also included gathering food and securing the mound from predators, as well as from nature, and protecting the baby ants from the same elements. One of the most standard characteristics of these ants was that they can lift almost twenty times their body mass. To put that in perspective, this would be the equivalent of a child being able to pick up a 200-pound digital piano.

These red fire ants across from Oscar had never been known to be very pleasant. Unlike other fire ant colonies that were very friendly and, in most cases, would get along well with other ant species, these red fire ants preferred to stay around their home alone. They would wait by themselves, even at the invitation of other ants within and from different colonies, to get together for whatever reason which was encouraged and practiced . Perhaps this resulted from a general mistrust the ants had of all the lizards and other creatures lurking and planning to eat any of the ants.

These fire ants shared a yard with some professional leaf-cutting ants and were the go-to for home repairs and remodeling. These leaf-cutting ants also included the two close friends, Eric and Roger. Their reputation has earned them the nickname ER, just short for their initials, and whenever you saw one, the other was close behind.

In gatherings such as picnics or at any meetings, the first name anyone would think of in terms of organizing was that of ER. They loved the spotlight. Wherever there was a crowd, regardless of the reason or occasion, ER could be counted upon to be front and center for attention, doing all they could to extend their fifteen minutes. The two had been friends since childhood and were now even closer because they lived in the same mound. When they were younger, they were often seen walking to school together. Sometimes, one would stay over at the other one's place. If it got too dark by the time they finished their homework and studied for the day, they would have dinner and spend the night there, whether at one of their places or the others. Not being together at one or the other's houses would cause concern for their parents. They often played games for the same team and on the playground in school.

27

One of the main things ER was well known for was their ability to work well with other ants, regardless of which mound or colony the other ants came from. These were the two guys to contact if you ever wanted to discover what was happening in and around the various mounds. Whenever there was an issue or dispute, regardless of who brought it up, if it interested or affected the other ants, ER would be the first to get right on it.

They were masters of social media. These two would use social media to spread information in and around the various mounds and had the unique ability to organize everything from celebrations to protests. ER was always instrumental in placing placards in various strategic locations to keep everyone informed of the happenings in and around the world of the mounds.

Yes, when times called for organizing friendships and socializing, they were the go-to team for that and all of the games. Regarding logistics, these leaf-cutting ants, in general, could accomplish feats that no other ants could imagine. One of the favorite games among all the leaf-cutting ants was the art-inspired cutting shapes out of the leaves. Known locally as shape cutter, it was a simple game, and the rules of this game were also simple. To begin, they could have a team of two or four ants, and they would not all have to come from the same mound. A coin flip determined the start. One ant would call out an object, and it would be up to the other ant to chew through a leaf in the object's shape or a word just mentioned by the opposing team, who would also start the timer. Part of the rules, though, stated that one ant could only call out a single item, such as a horse or a fly; complicated objects, such as a crowd of people or waterfalls, could not be used. Of course, all of this cutting by the ant would have to be done promptly. You could gain many points if you worked by yourself, but if you were part of a team, you would still earn points, though not as many as if you were playing by yourself.

The winner would get points for speed and completion of the finished picture, and it must look genuine, as it is to be judged by the opposing team. Negotiations could begin if there was a disagreement among the perceived winner on the opposing team, and points values could go up or down.

Once you won any amount of points, these were points that they could carry over with you or to another team. If they left their current team or the winning individuals, they decided to compete alone or somewhere else, and the points would go accordingly. To officiate in the game, an ant would always find a neutral body, someone not participating, preferably an older member of the mound, or they would judge each other's work. Often, it was simply ER who did all of the judging.

ER did not necessarily think of themselves as more intelligent or better than any other leaf-cutting ants. Still, everyone knew they were at least more creative, social, and outspoken. As far as their age was concerned, they would be the equivalent of an adult male in their upper twenties to early thirties. Even at that age, ER would present themselves as the go-to know-it-alls. They would even be the ones to go to for someone needing a recommendation for a handyman or repair guy, and they were considered the wise elders among the leaf-cutting ants. For this, their presence would always command attention, not only for their free-spirited mannerisms but also for their ability to articulate whatever point they or anyone needed to get across, and they would always offer a solution.

This was particularly helpful when they were in school together, as most other leaf-cutting ants would approach them to discuss an issue. These were issues that often were in the minds of ER and amounted to nothing more than gossip.

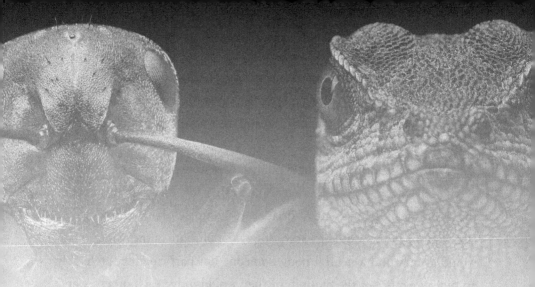

*T*oday was a day that Oscar had heard just about enough of Penni's recent nagging. Although Penni's nagging was done in jest, it was not just about the leaves but some of the essential cosmetic changes around the house that she felt had been neglected as of late—items such as the small paint patch on the front door near the handle, which needed to be retouched.

Oscar knew the paint color was something other than what they had stored at the house. There were also the boxes with some of Oscar's and their son, Gene's, stuff, items that neither of them no longer used, and these items needed to go into the garage, along with other knick-knacks that needed to go into the basement. Penni would phrase her comments as tidbits that needed some of Oscar's attention. Still, lately, she had mentioned them specifically by name and more often.

Despite it being James Bond Day, Oscar decided that today he would get started on one of these projects, and this meant he had to get out his new wireless blower from the garage; this is the new blower he bought recently but had yet to open and use. Each time he thought he would use it, he would consider, *Well, I also need to get this and that done.* In that moment of hesitation, something much more urgent always came up. But after putting it off for so long, and with considerable success each time, mainly by making empty promises for the past two weekends, he was more relaxed today, Saturday. He could postpone watching some of his Bond films until later. Then, he could finally get to watch them when he had the time, but now he wanted to get some of these chores done.

Tomorrow, Sunday, was the day for church, which Oscar and Penni would never miss, and the church service was followed by the usual socializing brunch with their fellow worshippers. Of course, this was more of an occasion for Penni to catch up on the latest gossip from and about the people she doesn't even like. Later in the day on Sunday, of course, in the afternoon, there was always the football game, and that was where Oscar would get his information about the people in the houses he was interested in buying from the other guys in the neighborhood. This would be information gathered, such as how far behind this or that person was on a mortgage and who might be interested in moving or selling. This social get-together often would run into the early evening and dinner time. The information that Oscar would gather could be gained over a card game or dominos.

Oscar sometimes used these routines on Sundays to finish any Bond films he'd started the previous day but could not finish because something came up or he fell asleep during the broadcast. Today would be the first time he would test his new gas-powered handheld blower, which used regular gasoline. His old blower had a mechanical malfunction a while back. That malfunction became one of those situations where buying a new blower was less expensive than buying the parts to try and repair the old one. The combination of time and money made it cost-prohibitive; besides that, with the old blower, the fuel had to be mixed with an oil additive each time before it was used. Oscar could never leave the oil inside the old blower, as it would clog the valves, making it impossible for him to start it the next time he wanted to use it.

Oscar hated the two-step process, and that's one of the main reasons

31

things fell behind. In Oscar's mind, that was one of his main excuses for not getting the leaves done sooner. If he could get away with it, he would prefer to light a fire under all the dead leaves, burning them and anything that he could fit on top of the leaves. This might include all old furniture, clothing, and anything under the leaves, such as trash and newspapers. However, the city's strict fire code and the HOA's policies made this a non-option. Knowing the kind of neighbors and his relationship with some of them, someone would snitch if he wanted to start an unauthorized fire.

Over by the Becks, leaves accumulated directly in front of their house, where they also had their trash. This made it ideal for rummaging raccoons and squirrels, especially if the bags were left open, and Oscar and Penni noticed this.

Penni once thought one could tell much about someone just by being nosey and pawing through their trash. Some of the fundamental discoveries of going through the trash may include answering basic questions about the household, questions as to whether they were male or female, and how old he or she was. Maybe even if they had kids, how old those kids were, and of what gender.

Going through the trash, you can also speculate about what kind of work they did, what sort of things they bought and discarded, the condition of these discarded items, the junk mail they received which was eventually tossed out, the kind of books or magazines, if any, they read. In some cases, going through the trash would also reveal how well off they were by examining the kind of food they ate, whether it be the bargain store brands or the premium brands, and how much of it they discarded and when it was discarded to the best "if used by" date.

The Kyrie family of ants lived in Mr. Mark's yard, a yard many of the other ant colonies would consider a safe location, as Mr. Mark was a single person who, in particular, did not do a lot of yard work. A lot of gardening, yes, but the Kyrie family was embedded somewhere deep in the cracks between the concrete slabs, substantially deeper than other ant colonies in the neighborhood. They were well dug into what they thought was far enough in the ground and outside of plain view since the space between each slab of concrete sank much deeper below the surface than any other ant colony. However, unlike Oscar's yard, there was no water hose that allowed random amounts of water to run down the front driveway of Mr. Mark's household.

Their thought processes also differed from the ants in Oscar's yard. The ones in Oscar's yard thought that even by using the powerful new blower, Oscar would not harm them, at least not by much. It was widely believed that the powerful new blower would be better than the old one—better by blowing and, in effect, redepositing some sand back onto the top of their sanctuary, saving them all the time and energy needed to transport the sand to a new location to rebuild any of the destroyed mounds or any part of the foundation that came undone by either water or heavy winds.

Oscar had often noted that he could see who he believed to be his neighbor's water wasting away. By this, he referred primarily to Mr. Mark's water running down the sidewalk and into the street. But with no visible water hoses in sight, no one, not even Penni, was still determining where he got those ideas. One can easily dismiss this as pure propaganda, his spreading rumors designed to get the votes of the other residents on his side for the HOA meeting. This would be a feat, though, as Mr. Mark's water hose was located on the side of their house, at an angle facing away from Oscar's house, and not in the front, like the hose on Oscar's home.

Oscar said he could tell that Mr. Mark wasted water, and Oscar knew this even with the water hose positioned directly on the side and out of his immediate view. Oscar once said to Penni that he was 100% sure Mr. Mark did not tighten the hose to its nozzle enough, and now he said he thought the hose and nozzles on Mr. Mark's house needed to be replaced. These were all observations Oscar claimed to have made when he visited the house a while back, when he, Penni, and Mr. Mark were on regular speaking terms.

Although Oscar and Mr. Mark were not strangers or even hostile to each other, the extent of their interactions and exchanges were confined primarily to the once-in-a-while royal hand wave. Usually, but not often, it was accompanied by a simple greeting of, "good morning," "good evening," or "good night." This was done with the instantly generated smiles of both individuals who were making the greetings.

Like most men in his age group, Mr. Mark, a retired police officer by profession, loved to mind his own business and never took to anyone saying something that he felt was being dictated to him. This included their opinion of him or what they thought he should do about any matter, such as his family, house, or yard. Mr. Mark lived alone in his house. On any given day, if he had been seen outside of his home, it would be to go for the newspaper or one of his long walks and sometimes the occasional washing of his car. He never had visitors coming by his house, and almost every time, the only person seen coming from his home was the mailman or some other delivery person; Oscar and Penni never inquired about his relationship status. Nor did he volunteer any indication or information in any past conversation.

In Oscar's mind, the ants and lizards in his surroundings were only confined to his yard. At worst, he thought it was some conspiracy or voodoo magic that was directed towards him and his family. The thing with Oscar was, in his mind, if you see one of these vermin, primarily the ants, that indicated there were many, many, more just waiting in the wings, waiting for the chance to get into his home and deliberately destroy everything.

And with many more vermin waiting out of view, they were almost sure to have eggs. However, regarding the ants, the queen is the only one that can lay eggs. When these eggs hatch, the new ants would create a new colony. Depending on the kind of ant, some, but not all, will build their colonies underground, and some will build elaborate structures standing tall above ground. And that's when they become visible and a nuisance to homeowners like Oscar. On some occasions, when surveying his yard, he did come across some of these masterpieces rising slightly above the grass.

As far as Liz was concerned, she and Lee would encounter Oscar primarily when viewing him passing by, albeit occasionally, with his grandkids and sometimes his dog, a light and dark brown German shepherd named Blondi, but that was mainly on the weekends, but not this weekend.

Liz considered her day officially begun when one of a few things happened. One was Oscar turning on the water hose on a day like today, and the other was just after a drizzle of rain. Liz always made it a priority to start every day with a fresh drink of cool or room temperature water, no matter what the source of that water was, but drinking from this dripping water spot was by far one of her favorite places, providing some cool, fresh water.

Whenever water was turned on, Oscar would wield the hose with the force of a tsunami-like wave to wash down his driveway. The ground would start shaking, like drums beating in a military-style parade, growing louder. The water temperature would rise by the seconds as it advanced towards the mounds.

Lee and the rest of his family would begin to notice small cracks inside the walls of the mound as soon as the running water hit the sides of the mound, starting at the base. The makeshift pillars holding up the mound would, in small pieces, begin to come apart from the outside and work their way to the inside of the living quarters of the ants.

Curious, Lee had always been the bravest and by far the most outgoing in his mound, and usually, he would be among the first to go out and see what all the commotion caused by the water flow was about. Like the other male ants and the queen, Lee was one of the ants with wings, so he could fly around, watch from above, and report back to the others if needed. The workers who built the mound did not have wings. The male ants' job was primarily to mate with the queen. Once they do, they do not live much longer. However, depending on the species, a single colony can have many queens. Still, once the queen grows into adulthood, her lifespan is spent laying eggs.

Although Lee had been through this kind of crisis and survived a few times before, it was always exciting and sometimes surreal to him to see how the other ants reacted to the shaking and systematic minor destruction of the various parts of the mound. For Lee, it was like the feeling people get when they live in high-risk areas for hurricanes. Everything is all about preparation. They have been through this kind of destruction so often that they have learned to accept it.

Unfortunately for Lee and the rest of his vast family, ants did not have lungs to breathe, so being submerged in water for an extended time can prove deadly. For them, the oxygen they live in and the carbon dioxide they exhale enter and exit their body through the same tiny holes throughout their body.

Lee was walking to project his sense of bravery, his chest puffed out, and he boldly turned his head, looking from side to side along the way. Whenever the water started running more intensely, many other ants, workers, and all, would be heading for cover, running, screaming, and holding their heads for protection from the falling debris. Some even grabbed their young ones and their significant others by whatever body part was most accessible at the moment to continue their escape.

A flow of lukewarm water was flooding the mound; any frail, disabled, or otherwise unfortunate ants caught off guard in the water's path would have to try and hold onto whatever they could. Some were holding onto the walls, with their fingernails dug into the wall; this sounded like fingernails scraping a school blackboard. These ants were just beneath the water's surface, where, from here, they could only hold their breath for a few seconds at most. Most of the ants had that feeling because the water was not at room temperature; they had nothing to fear, but it shocked them because it was a bit cold initially. Lukewarm water would not have provided a jolt, but it is still better for the body, at least in the short term. With that steady water flow becoming more pronounced, once the water had covered them and they had to hold their breath even for a few seconds, they would easily drown and wash away.

Lee paused, looking at what parts of the mound crumbled the fastest; he could tell the damage was minimal. Flying up the wall from where he was on the ground, Lee could hear the drumming of the water as the flow increased and got closer and louder. From his vantage point, he initially thought the water flow sounded more like the stomping of millions of ant feet. To him, it was reminiscent of the first *Jurassic Park* movie scene, with each impact-generating vibration getting louder than the previous one, and one could see the ripples in the standing water. From above, Lee could see Liz approaching him in the same direction as the water flowed, and she was casually walking. Liz was undeterred by the volume of water or the ants she could see in the distance, all running for cover.

As she picked up the pace, with each step she took, the impact generated by the sound and slam of her feet would splash, and the water would reach above her body. Although unintentionally, her splash would hit the walls of the mound and cause even more sand to crumble off the walls, washing away additional parts of the mound. But with each step, as the water flow hit her feet, it provided some friction and slowed down the process as she walked along.

Lee's eyes were fixed on Liz, but not out of fear. The sudden fear of seeing any other lizard sometimes paralyzed him temporarily. He flew toward the ground and landed in one of the only dry spaces he could've found to touchdown.

Liz stood straight up once she approached and stood in front of Lee. He looked around the still crumbling mound, but between the two of them, nothing was said. Despite the sad and confused look on his and Liz's faces, neither Lee nor Liz would utter a word.

Unlike other ants that would have found themselves in this situation where they were standing before a giant lizard, Lee was not visibly trembling, even though the warm water hitting him was sure to cover him. He knew Liz would not let him get washed away to drown if the water became too much for him to bear. Liz looked at Lee and his surroundings, first to his left, then to the right. Lee's eyes matched her every eye movement; it was as if Lee was anticipating Liz to say something, and maybe she was waiting for him to speak.

When Liz lowered her head, she extended her dewlap, then raised her head again with her eyes fixed on Lee. Without either of them saying a word, Liz put her head down and started drinking some water. Then suddenly, she stopped; she raised her head as another ant went swimming by where she was drinking.

Still frozen on the inside, Lee did not move. If he was scared, he managed to cover it up very well; at least he thought so, as if he expected her to raise her head after the first drink or—even after seeing that ant swim by in her path, say something that was not threatening but at least inspirational. The fact that he knew her made the predicted outcome to be that of the latter.

Under normal circumstances, any ant that sees a lizard walk or run towards them would immediately think the lizard was about to eat them whole. According to the laws of nature and based on historical accounts of their individual species' past encounters, these two creatures, Liz and Lee, were not supposed to be friends or even trust each other. Still, the relationship between these two was different.

It was awkward at first. When the two first met, Liz was on one of her regular walks when she approached a lizard that had passed on at the hands of Vergil. This lizard was walking near the steps of the house when Vergil sprang up from what the ants thought was just a catnap. Vergil pounced; both front paws landed on the lizard's tail, and the lizard's head rose up and into Vergil's mouth, resulting in what they now saw before them.

Around this lizard were hundreds of thousands of ants, eating away at what was left of that lizard. Liz paused, looking at the ants having their feast at ground level. When she glanced over to the hill, Lee was sitting on the mountain alone, not partaking in the feast. Liz walked over to Lee, and he did not run away from her. She asked him why he was sitting alone and not joining the feast. Lee told her he did not want to participate in the feast as he knew the lizard. Liz didn't ask him specifically about the friendship with the Gila monster that had passed.

Lee began to tell Liz he was passing by, and that is when he saw his friend, Maxine, a Gila monster, get decapitated. He said the two of them were conversing, and that's when Vergil, the Beck's cat, passed by. Lee said he was standing beside her rear legs when Virgil reached down and grabbed Maxine by her head. Lee said he felt helpless. He could not save his long-lost friend. Virgil had one paw on Maxine's back, as he began to chew his way through her. Gila monsters are venomous, so by the time Vergil got to her stomach, he paused. This is when I believe the venom had gotten to him. He moved his head back and forth rapidly, making a sound similar to a hairball couch. Then he vomited the parts of Maxine he had just eaten. Lee went on to say that at that point, he just sat there with the remains of his friend as Vergil ran off. Soon after, all the ants started gathering and eating what was left of Maxine.

Lee and Liz sat there next to each other and conversed about things of general interest, such as what it takes to keep their families and friendships alive despite the challenges. Although this conversation occurred two years ago, Lee and Liz have always been friends.

They became even closer friends when Liz walked back with Lee to his mound that same day, and another lizard approached him. That random lizard did not look at or try to eat Lee with Liz by his side. And that's how it's been ever since. The two of them were almost like a mismatched couple who first met online and were now meeting each other face to face. Or an odd couple being put together for the first time, as in one of those reality shows perhaps set in a shelter. Now, they are trying to make sense of the situation and their surroundings, particularly after losing everything in some disaster.

Lee could breathe and stand without trembling, as the volume of water at this level was something he had previously experienced. For now, his head was still above water. Liz paused, looked down at Lee, and blinked once.

Again, extending her dewlap, she looked into Lees' eyes and asked with a smile, "How are you holding up?"

It was not a question due to the water flow but rather one based on the morning's overall events. Lee responded with a few nods of his head up and down, turning his head side to side while keeping his mouth closed as if to say he was doing fine. Still, he was thinking and feeling otherwise.

"It's a sad day for all of us," Liz continued. "This has happened too many times before and way too often in these particular parts."

Lee nodded twice in agreement. This was part of the nonverbal communication that Liz and Lee had grown used to when they were together. It was more Liz who had taught Lee, but he caught on fast and had learned quite a bit since they first met.

That calm Lee and Liz were momentarily experiencing was now interrupted. Suddenly, a sound began reverberating like a helicopter getting closer. Liz looked up in the distance, towards the direction of the mysterious sound coming from behind her. She could see the falling leaves in a stampede, approaching them. Seeing this, Lee reinforced his balance by sinking his feet firmly into the ground. However, what was beginning to feel like an earthquake was growing stronger. The leaves rolled towards them like flying razors, bouncing up and down as they zoomed by. Lee thought this was most likely not an earthquake but more of a tornado, as it was clearing away the rest of his home and leaving behind a lot of debris scattered about the yard. Liz dipped her head and then tilted it to the left, signaling to Lee that it was time to go, or at least it was time to get out of harm's way.

Lee did not immediately move; part of that decision was out of fear, and the other was pure curiosity. He was curious to see what would happen next to his home, what would become of his friends and family, and what was left of his surroundings. He feared that if he left, he would be unable to help anyone he thought needed help.

Liz extended her throat again and turned to the left, using her whole body, signaling Lee to move. Liz insisted that Lee take immediate action. With a more robust, warm breeze, the leaves were blowing past Lee, and with a closer look, Lee could see some other ants approaching in the wind, some unable to hold on, and others surfing on the backs of maple tree leaves, punching a hole with their hands and feet into the leaves for balance. The leaves were flipping over and rolling about, but the ants on top of these leaves somehow managed—although barely—to hang on.

Lee looked up and saw that it was Oscar with his powerful new leaf blower, and he was gliding it along, sweeping from side to side. With every two steps Oscar took forward, he would take one back and then forward twice again, blowing the leaves out of his path and towards the road in front and away from him. As the wind from the blower grew more intense, it felt warmer with each step and swing from Oscar. It was as if a jet engine was directly in front of them, and he could feel the G force when the plane was getting ready to take off.

Although Oscar may not have aimed explicitly for ants, he could see their mound in his path. Oscar was now smiling as he thought of these ants as nothing more than a bunch of frustrating vermin that needed to be exterminated anyway. He had been trying to devise new ways to get rid of them and prevent more of them from setting up camp anywhere, especially from reaching the doorway of his house, let alone into it. Oscar had made it his life's mission to get rid of them in any way he possibly could, and by any means possible, ever since he first discovered them in his yard while doing his hard work.

With Liz and Lee standing directly in the path of the approaching wind, the pressure from the blower, combined with the amount of debris it kicked up along the way, was becoming increasingly violent. The force was getting too much for any creature to bear and too much to ignore anymore. At this point, even Liz began to slip.

Looking ahead, Liz saw a rolling stampede in the distance. Many ants not on leaves could now be seen running, rolling, and falling over each other, coming in the same direction as the approaching noise and wind. On the outer parts of the mound, leaves and ants were blown around and falling very far and fast. Ants were flying, hitting the leaves, bouncing up and down and off the ground, trying to hold on to anything at arm's length, and ripping off pieces of the mound and some of their body parts, such as antennas, along the way.

Barely holding on, it seemed as though Lee and Liz were the only two left unscathed, remaining in the path of what to them was now similar to a tornado. Liz walked over and stopped in front of Lee. She bent her head down again to the ground, but this time, she verbally told Lee to climb onto her back. This time, Lee did not hesitate; his eyes widened. He flapped his wings, leaped onto Liz's back, and grabbed the tiny cleft on her head as he sat on Liz's head. He did it all so fast that once he sat down, he realized his head was facing toward what was now behind them. Leaves were still flying past, on top, and all around them. Liz took off running. The wind behind her back and Lee's face felt like she was moving faster than ever. Liz said the force of the wind pushed her, almost carrying her, and indeed it did.

What took mere seconds of her fast running, to her mind, felt like it lasted forever. Finally, Liz stopped and went to the shaded side, behind a solid rock planted firmly into the ground and out of Oscar's path. She thought she could stand there for a while to catch her breath, if nothing else, and wait for this storm to pass. Lee, who was still sitting on her back after the wild ride—with so many turns in that short run—welcomed the break. Even though Liz was reasonably athletic, running that far and as fast as they could move while trying not to lose Lee on her back was something she was not used to doing. The running she'd been used to doing was short jogs, and those were just for exercise.

Looking around, Lee and Liz caught their breath as they reviewed the path they had just run. Not only was the entire mound flat, but all the various family memories and mementos on the walls inside the mound were scattered way beyond the yard's boundaries and in multiple directions.

Liz and Lee knew they could not stand behind this rock forever. Even though Oscar had stopped swerving for a few minutes, they knew he would eventually start walking towards them again. The wind was still noticeably heavy for these few minutes, and Oscar was still standing with the blower turned on. They knew that eventually, it would catch up to them, and perhaps that would be when—and not if—Oscar decided to start walking forward again and continue cleaning around the rock as well.

Liz made the misstep of going out again in the path of the wind from behind the rock to test the strength of the breeze, and as soon as she did, she was instantly overcome by a strong current. She was spun over and onto her side. Despite this fumble, Lee did manage to hold on, and the two rolled over and over in sync several times before stopping about two feet from the rock where they'd started.

With ants scattered throughout the yard and around Lee and Liz, it was apparent that the wind did get to most of the ants, hiding in places such as between the cracks of the wall. Some ants were still holding onto the leaves. Although those ants holding onto the wall between the cracks were partially sheltered, it became apparent to Lee and Liz that they could not hold on indefinitely. This ordeal seemed to last an eternity, but it only took a few seconds.

The entire mound and all the ants were scattered around the yard and along the front side of the house. Many ants appeared as if they were intoxicated, fumbling, and stumbling about without any sense of direction.

Some tried to stand up, but this proved difficult as many had lost at least one leg. At the same time, some were holding their heads and backs and looking around at the path they would typically take to get back and forth to the mound. Perhaps they were looking around to see if they could find that lost limb, but that path was now just a memory.

Little to nothing remained to remind them of where they came from or where they needed to go. With no queen visible to set the agenda, give new orders, or tell them what needed to get done first, second, or third, it was every ant for him or herself caught up in chaos, and every ant was left to wander about aimlessly.

Liz still had her balance and could stand up once more with Lee still on her back. Once she rose, she shook her head aggressively like a wet dog, but not to the point where it would knock Lee off her back. Some ants hiding between the cracks throughout this came out and walked in the same path that Oscar and his blower had just covered. Oscar was beginning to walk about, stepping on many of the wandering ants, a move that, at first, to Liz and Lee, appeared to be deliberate, and maybe it was. But then, a few seconds later, Oscar stopped and turned off the blower long enough for Lee and Liz to use the break to catch their breath quickly. Liz turned her head towards Lee and asked him if he was doing okay.

Lee was fine; at that moment, he just had a thought. He said he could recall the previous year when Oscar was standing in this spot, and he planted what the ants thought was ant food. That day, which had started just like the one before, was just a boring midmorning. Oscar was tired of the creatures throughout his yard, and although all the ants did not want to trust him, some still thought the food he had laid out on the ground was a goodwill jester.

"But I always thought maybe it was something more sinister, like he just wanted all of us and them eliminated," Lee told her.

It was not unusual for Oscar to be up this late in the day, let alone be out in the yard, as he liked to get his yard work done before the sun became somewhat unbearable. However, the situation was insufficient to start gossiping or even raising casual suspicions. As ants, they were used to feeding on Oscar's trash.

Items such as the half-eaten bagel or the last few drops of his morning latte that would linger in the discarded cup and other little surprises were always on the menu. Whenever Oscar brought out the trash, he tied the trash bags at the top, using the twist ties to secure them very tight before tossing them into the dumpster. Still, that day, he did not do any of that. Once in a while, a bag would leak out some of the liquid, along with leftover food, plus things such as half-eaten fruits that ants and lizards could feed on. These were the most common items that would fall out of the leaking bags. When liquid leaks from the trash bag and onto the ground, Oscar seldom uses a water hose to wash it away. Sometimes, he lets it sit there and dry up, knowing that one of his many vermin will eat it. Or he waits for the rain to come and wash it away. If left up to the ants, they would often form a queue extending from the yard's entrance and proceeding to his front door and down the driveway. This was easily visible to Oscar; sometimes, the queue would extend into the trash receptacle, where Oscar would always notice them and get annoyed.

That day, when Oscar was walking around his yard, he noticed that there seemed to be many more ant mounds. Lee said that Oscar strategically placed a sweet strawberry-like smelling red liquid inside a fast-food drink cup lid and placed the lid very noticeably in front of his house. Rod, the second cousin to Lee and a very muscular and adventurous young fire ant from across the road, was one of the first ants to notice this. Rod can usually be found in the Beck's yard, where he spends much of his time. He was dating someone who lived there and was the first to get to the food. The smell attracted him, so he instantly spread the news to all the other fire and leaf-cutting ants. He was usually not on this side of the road, let alone in this yard, but today, however, he was walking by, visiting his family on the other side when he noticed the food and was the first to

45

approach it. He also became the first to climb over the top of the lid and slide down the edge to investigate the sweet-smelling red substance. The smell of the thick syrup-like drink was temptation's best friend; it looked irresistibly sweet and sticky.

As word quickly spread, a few more dozen ants came by, and one after the other, they felt the temptation from the smell, and none could resist the urge to take just one taste. No, for these ants, the samples required second and third dips. Word traveled quickly, and the ants were not the only ones to be contacted and to sample the treat; a few of the lizards passing by also indulged, as they were eager to join the impromptu picnic.

On the surface, the day seemed to be just another beautiful day, and it was indeed the start of another wonderful day for both the ants and lizards. It presented both ants and lizards with a chance to get together and talk about the issues that united them, all the while enjoying a meal together. Word quickly spread through the grapevine. So many ants were in attendance that their sheer volume could be seen from looking out the window of Oscar's house. No one ever stopped to notice if Oscar was looking at them, and at this moment, perhaps no one cared. The excellent time they had feasting lasted several minutes. The ants returned with some of the substance to their nest and shared it with their queen, who didn't consume any; instead, she passed it on to some of her workers. The frantic pace of taking the food back and forth lasted until all of the substance was gone.

Many ants were fatigued and had to stop and rest, which was unusual considering how energetic these ants typically are. Because the feast was so good, no one thought anything of it. Soon, many more of the ants were stopping to take that rest. Then, what began as a bit of rest turned into a power nap, an unusual power nap because there were so many participants. Usually, after a heavy meal, the elder ants would nod off first. Even solid and healthy ants like Rod needed to relax. Many dismissed this tiring feeling as justified because the food was too sweet, causing a sugar crash.

But soon, to a few, and then many, what became evident was that this so-called power nap had become permanent. The few lizards at the feast experienced the same fate. However, for the lizards, the pace at which they were dropping off made it necessary to stop. But that realization was much slower for the ants.

It took less than an hour to consume all of the great-smelling liquid, and this time, they included something to take back to the mound to show and share with the others. Dozens and dozens of ants and a few lizards lay there in the same spot, motionless and lifeless. One ant who did not participate in the feast was Lee. Lee said that when he approached all these ants and the lizard lying there motionless, he glanced through Oscar's window, where he could see Oscar standing and smiling. The mass poisoning was just another small victory for Oscar.

That event will always and forever remain one of the darkest events in the ants' and some lizards' memories, and it touched everyone. Relatives, friends, and whole families were gone, and everyone knew at least somebody lost in that event.

It is an event passed on from those who knew about it firsthand and then used it as a teaching tool in school for the many different generations of ants and lizards that would follow. Lee said this incident should be a warning, a lesson that each should teach one another within their respective communities. Many ants from across the street who did not join this feast still think of this incident as an urban legend.

Liz was one of those lizards that had no recollection of that event, but she did admit that she had heard of what had happened on that day; she said she always thought that it just meant that some of the ants and lizards were resting there motionless. Although she admitted, she did believe the part where they said that Oscar could be seen through his window, dancing and clapping his hands.

Suddenly, Lee's retelling of those horrific events was interrupted when screams were heard between the loud crunching of limbs breaking off the still-moving ants. Those who managed to be lucky enough to escape the blower now faced instant burial with each seemingly deliberate step and crunch as Oscar's feet stomped down indiscriminately. Oscar would raise his feet high in the air, then deliberately bring them down hard, twisting his feet with each step, smashing the ants while twisting them from side to side as he walked on them, turning many into an instant paste. Liz climbed back up and ran behind a slab of concrete just outside the reach of the blower and Oscar's feet, with Lee sitting on her back again, but this time, Lee was facing forward.

Liz then took off running. She stopped when she approached the stairs to Oscar's kitchen and climbed it, and from this vantage point, high up on the wall, Lee and Liz could quickly look down and see everything happening below.

The ear-to-ear smile on Oscar's face, the look of the soppy blend of smashed ants from the mass destruction, compiled with the scattering of the injured and mourning ants in pain, was laid out in plain view below them. For Lee and his family and friends, this was pain from not only the loss of their home but also from the inability to help and the impossibility of replacing the loved ones they had already lost and now dealing with the additional ones they were about to lose. The mass loss of life and the sounds of screaming coming from the survivors were overwhelming. Lee covered his ears, knowing he was helpless and could not comfort his brothers and sisters. Everyone needed either a drink of water, a hug, or words of encouragement; Liz and Lee knew they could not help any of them, and they both felt defeated.

Then there was silence for a moment when suddenly, Oscar stopped not just the blower but also stopped walking. Something in the corner of his view caught his attention. He turned slowly in that direction and instantly realized he had identified the most prominent mound's location. He could see some ants still running around between the pavement cracks. It was like last year when he saw this many ants everywhere. Oh yes, and then it occurred to him that it was the time he used the red liquid ant bait to get rid of them. The last time, he was hoping they would never return, at least not so quickly and not at this volume.

He thought, this time seeing that they found their way back into his yard in such vast numbers, he would have to seek a more drastic course of action. Since he didn't have any more of the red ant food he used before, this time, he would have to be much more creative.

Oscar laid down the blower, placed one hand on his hip, scratched his head with the other, and did deep, silent breathing. Still rubbing his head with one hand, Oscar looked around as if thinking of a final solution to rid his surroundings of this infestation. Still, he was like a writer suffering from writer's block.

The remaining ants walking around were way too many for him to step on. He thought he would miss too many of them, and they would scatter as soon as Oscar started stepping, effectively getting away before he could get to all of them. To add to his dilemma, he needed to be in better shape to keep up with running or more aggressive stamping. Oscar paused, turned around, and started to walk back toward the shed without the blower in his hand.

Liz and Lee remained calm, trying their best not to move a muscle, fearing what might happen if they did something stupid to draw attention. Luckily, they were overlooked. They stood silent, wondering what was to come next from Oscar. Oscar entered his shed, but Liz thought he would be there only for a few minutes, as the blower was still outside turned off.

Lee and Liz could hear the rumbling of things shifting around coming from inside the shed. It was as if he were searching for something specific. The noise was nothing they could recognize; whatever he picked up and put back down did not make a sound that Liz and Lee were familiar with. None of the ants or lizards knew or could think what he might be searching for, and perhaps none of them wanted to know.

A few moments of patient waiting passed, and the rumbling of whatever

Oscar was searching for stopped. Oscar came walking out of the shed, but this time whistling, with a red canister in one hand and flipping a small silver object in the other hand. He would toss the silver object and catch it while whistling and walking. He continued walking toward where he had left the blower.

At first, Liz and Lee thought the blower ran out of fuel, as the writing on the side of the red canister in Oscar's hand was the word, "GAS." As Liz and Lee waited patiently, anticipating what Oscar was up to, the air relaxed as if the temperature suddenly changed. A hint of fear raised goosebumps over Lee's and Liz's bodies as Oscar's shadow covered them. Lee and Liz watched curiously as Oscar bent down and refilled the blower. Fearing that he was about to restart the machine and continue where he had left off, they thought he would see them or at least come in their direction, so they did not move.

Oscar poured some of the fuel into the blower slowly, but he was not looking directly at the canister and the blower and did not realize what he was doing; some of the fuel spilled over the side of the blower on the ground when the blower was filled up to the top. Oscar looked at his error and instantly raised the canister, spilling even more of the fuel. Oscar then saw that the spilled fuel that had poured out of the sides had fallen onto some of the ants, who were now struggling to walk.

Liz and Lee watched this from the sidelines, and Lee could hear the screams of the ants when the fuel was poured down onto them. Liz and Lee could see the instant burn marks on the ants. Oscar paused. A million things could have been running through Oscar's head, but the look on Oscar's face was emotionless. No smile or anger. It was almost as if he did not want to know and did not care about what was happening to these ants. As he watched this unfold, the struggling ants suddenly stopped moving one by one. Oscar began to rise to his feet; he had a slowly growing grin on his face. He seemed satisfied that he suddenly had a bright new idea. It was as if a light had been turned on, and he was steering directly into that light.

He reached back into his pocket and pulled out the silver thing in his hand: a coin, a quarter. He would flip it up in the air, catch it with the same hand, and slam it down on the back of his other hand, smiling.

With a grin, he said, looking down at the ground, "Well, I guess you lost."

Since he was without more of the red ant "food," Oscar thought he could now use the fuel to rid his yard of these unwanted "pests," the vermin. He did not have to drive far to get everything he needed. To his surprise, he found lots of fuel. Armed with the canister in hand, Oscar walked over to where the mound was, with the canister uncapped. He placed the canister near his nose to sniff the fuel better, making sure it was still fresh. Oscar did not frown or grin; his face had no sad or sorry expression. Looking down at the remaining ants, slowly at first, he began to pour, splattering the canister's contents onto the ants. After a small drip, the liquid became a steady stream. He moved his hands and feet forward and backward to cover the length of the many cracks in the pavement and made sure the fuel would flow through the cracks in the direction of the mound. He poured some of the remaining fuel onto the ants on the wall and in the slots, then turned his attention to the ants he could see still walking around until they also stopped moving. Oscar appeared proud as he bent down to look at the ants with fuel poured over them. He could see that their flesh had been burnt off the larger ants. And now, nothing but the exoskeletons of these ants remained.

The screams coming from the ants at first were sporadic but deafening, not just to Liz and Lee but also to the ants outside the path of this madman. As quickly as the ants' screams grew louder, they became quiet. In the blink of an eye, he had covered a large part of the yard, and all the remaining ants lying where he poured the fuel were now motionless and silent. Soon after, it became totally quiet as the horror of his act of eliminating the vermin netted an instant result.

Lee and Liz looked on from the sidelines with wide-open mouths. The running around of the ants was brief, as most only took a single step or two after the poison covered them, and then they would stop moving instantly.

A few moments later, the entire colony in between and on top of the concrete was silent, and the fuel running through the crack was now losing its potency. The wind carried the fumes far, which acted as a warning to the fire ants and lizards. Some of the other ants and the other creatures, like the lizards that were far away and up in the trees, could only look on in disbelief, as they were far enough away and standing at attention, but still fearful as to what Oscar's next move would be.

Oscar began to shake the canister, side to side and up and down, then peeked inside to investigate its remains. He wanted to ensure he had drained the last drop from the can and onto the ground, considering there were very few ants still walking around in his immediate vicinity. All of the lizards had kept their distance. There was no telling if Oscar was doing this to intimidate those whose locations he could not see. Oscar did want them to see him, and he was doing it to convey that there was a new way to rid his property of these pests and that more of this new way was to come. He would bend over, looking at the ground close up and around him to ensure he did not miss any ants between the cracks, including those sitting on the concrete. He searched, presuming some ants might just be lying there, playing dead or unconscious.

To reinforce whatever he was trying to convey, he held the canister up to his eye level, looking inside it while keeping the other eye as a lookout. He could see that every bit of fuel was now drained from the canister. Holding the canister back at his side, a look of satisfaction was quickly followed by one of disappointment. With the satisfaction that he had once again eliminated some of the vermin, plus the powerful sensation of discovering a new and more effective way to stop the ants, as well as the lizards or any other vermin that roam his yard, he smiled to himself and thought, that's life!

At the same time, he was disappointed that he'd run out of fuel so quickly and could not pour any more fuel specifically onto the points where vermin seemed to make their entry and exit every time they came back. Either way, a smiling Oscar looked down at where the mound was, content that he had gotten most of these vermin or at least got to send them a message that they were not welcome back on his property. Oscar walked back to the shed with the empty canister in hand, whistling and, once again, flipping the coin in the air. Lee and Liz were frozen still on top of their safety hideout.

Moments later, Oscar returned, but thankfully, he was empty-handed this time. He began to survey the area, including where Liz and Lee stood. Thankfully, he did not notice them still standing behind the rock. Oscar stood where he had laid down the blower earlier. With a bottle of water in one hand, he wiped the sweat from his forehead; with the outside of the cold bottle and the other on his hip, he twisted from side to side while standing stationary as if doing stretching and bending exercises.

Oscar stood and watched as the last bit of the gasoline evaporated from the pavement. Visually, he seemed satisfied with the day's work. Several feelings ran through both Liz's and Lee's heads. Among these were fear, hatred, anger, frustration, and sadness. All these simultaneously occupied both of their minds, and nothing within view could come to mind that would offer comfort or indicate a possible solution.

Liz slammed her fist onto the ground and told Lee she thought of jumping onto Oscar's back or neck, knowing that would scare him. She knew he was afraid of serpents and any other creature who caught him off guard at first, startling him and making his heart race. Liz says she can remember seeing that even when playfully with him, Penni once had a rubber snake as part of a Halloween gag gift. Oscar got very scared and jumped with his hands in the air, screamed, and then held his heart. But then Liz thought, if she did that, she was afraid that Oscar would swing his hands around and either knock her to the ground, step on her, or worse, pour something on her, just as he did earlier. Oscar would do anything to injure her in some way. Oscar would either hurt her or chase her to the point where she would become separated from her friends and family, perhaps even getting her cornered somewhere in the house. Then, he could move in for an attack and kill.

She also thought, well, if she indeed were to jump on top of him, then it would not just be her life that was in danger. She and Lee would be on the ground in his path so he could vent his anger fully and step on one or both of them. Liz said she feared that Lee at least might end up intentionally chased back inside the fuel path, and even though the fuel and the fumes from the smell were evaporating ever so slowly, sinking into the ground, they would accidentally inhale a lot of it and become paralyzed. Another situation was that Oscar could slap the back of his neck so hard that she and Lee would instantly break some of his bones against his body.

Lee thought he could also jump down and bite him on the neck, but then it occurred to him, as it did to Liz, that he would knock them off onto the ground, or Oscar would slap his neck as if he thought it was a mosquito. Lee felt that he could also end up decapitated and unable to help with the future rebuilding of the mound, so he dismissed those thoughts, as did Liz.

Oscar walked over and picked up the blower; he pulled on the starter string of the blower once, then a few times in quick repetition. Each pull left Liz and Lee opening their mouths wider as the fear of a blower restarting was anticipated. A few moments later, after several additional attempts, Oscar got the blower restarted. With Oscar holding the blower and pointing straight up into the sky, Lee and Liz's fears became a reality.

Oscar smiled and slowly lowered the blower. He pointed it toward the leaves in a pile at the end of the walkway. He started to clear away anything that lay on the ground down the path of his driveway towards the pile. This time around, he was walking away from where Liz and Lee were standing. With the blower in hand, he not only blew away the leaves but also all of the dead ants and lizards, pushing them into the same pile against the tree in the front of his yard, almost to the road. This tree stood on the opposite side of the yard from the rock on which Liz and Lee stood, clear across Oscar's front lawn.

Lee slowly climbed down onto the ground from off Liz's back. Once on the ground, each step was like walking on glass. It required one of them to be on the lookout not only for Oscar but also to make sure they did not step on the blood or remaining flesh that was burnt off from the fuel of a loved one who had recently passed or even one who was still breathing but was stuck to the ground, held there by their blood or pieces of their flesh like glue. They also had to be wary of Oscar potentially turning the blower back around again, but this time in their direction, something he would sometimes do if he felt he had missed one or two leaves that were blown about, courtesy of the wind.

As if there were not enough death and destruction around them to observe on their journey to the bottom, they were about to encounter another weird and downright unpleasant site. Once they got to the ground and started to walk away from the rock, Liz and Lee discovered what they thought had become the most horrific threat: two bearded dragon s lizards, from an original four where they were kept as pets by Oscar's son Gene, both very well-toned aggressive males.

Reptan and Crocod were standing in a face-to-face confrontation, a common occurrence when two lizards were about to fight or have a territorial dispute. They were staring at each other, nose to nose, with their dewlaps extending and retracting several times and raising their heads up and down with each extension. Lizards are reptiles, and that being said, their closest relative is that of a snake. There are some rare lizards, however, who, because they have no legs, do look like snakes. Just like snakes, lizards use their tongue to smell. However, these two bearded dragon lizards, Reptan and Crocod, did not fit those descriptions.

Liz said that in times of conflict and massive suffering, most will think it is time for everyone to unite. The old saying goes, "The enemy of my enemy is my friend." Lee nodded his head in agreement. Liz was still facing Lee when she said she was sure these two would have considered Oscar their enemy, not the ants or each other. Liz approached them gradually; she was unsure how they would react to seeing her as a female and having an ant with her as a friend. Or how they might respond, knowing that even though Lee was with her, she was not about to eat Lee as they might have thought. Liz approached both lizards from one side and stopped directly before them. She stared at them, and they turned to look at her.

By bopping their small heads and short necks up and down, this maneuver allowed one lizard to try to intimidate the other. In such a scenario, they will stare each other down to try and size each other up. Just like humans, lizards also have eyelids. Still, unlike humans, these eyelids, when they blink, have the purpose of protecting and cleaning their eyes, working like windshield wipers. Other types of lizards, those with no eyelids, use their tongue to achieve the same results, and their tongue also tells them the direction of food and helps them find a mate. Speaking of finding things, even though the lizards don't have ears, they do have eardrums, and these are located just below the surface of their skin, which makes their hearing not as good as that of humans but far superior to that of their relative, the snake.

After what Liz and Lee had just gone through, at least for the ants, they were unsure what these two could disagree about, so Liz and Lee continued cautiously approaching. Lizards usually fight by jumping on each other and sometimes rolling over each other, just like snakes do. These two were in the beginning stages, just before the start of jumping. Liz was glad she made it to them before actual contact had begun.

Liz moved toward them cautiously to talk to them without sounding like she was scolding or judging; without knowing any details of the disagreement, she began by speaking in a manner that sounded as if she was the long-lost friend who just wanted to find out what was happening.

So, Liz asked, "Gentlemen, what seems to be the problem?"

But before she could get an answer, both Reptan and Crocod stopped facing each other, lowered their heads, and turned towards Liz. Liz exhaled an energetic sigh of relief. There was now silence, not just between Reptan and Crocod, but primarily because Oscar had the blower turned off. If the walls of the mound could talk, with the blower now turned off, you could hear the sounds of whispers and cries from not only the ants but also the lizards; that's if there were any such sounds. If they did talk, there would be comments like, "Thank God," asking questions such as, "Was he finished?" and, "Is it now safe to wonder about the yard once again?"

Not knowing what would happen next only added to Liz and Lee's anxiety. Everyone hoped for the best; things could have been much worse in retrospect, considering how bad things were. It was a welcome relief to see Oscar walking back to his shed with blower in hand and leaving the scene. Liz and Lee once again turned their attention to Reptan and Crocod.

Reptan and Crocod approached each other again, presumably to pick up where they left off. This time with Liz and a few of the surviving wiser elders that had since joined to investigate the commotion and intervene if needed. Reptan and Crocod looked around and, seeing this many lizards around them, realized that they should not put on a show in front of them. Both then decided to step back and part ways by stepping away from each other and heading in opposite directions.

With Oscar now leaving the scene as well, it was a free-for-all. Reptan and Crocod saw that Oscar, Liz, and Lee had left, and what remained of the passerby lizards and ants were going in a different direction. Several dead ants' flesh was still on the ground, which made for instant meals for these two. They quickly ate up the small skin pieces stuck to the concrete.

As they were eating in what appeared to be a straight line, coming from different directions, their heads bumped while going after the same piece of dead ants in their paths. The two of them stopped. With plenty of food to go around, this led again to the face-to-face confrontation that Liz and Lee had just witnessed.

Hearing the grunts from their commotion, Liz stopped and turned around as she approached them again and began the conversation.

With a smile, Liz asked questions such as, "I thought we settled this already" and "How did you guys' day begin?" There was no immediate answer from either one of them. Liz asked, "How long have you two known each other?" and "Where did the two of you meet."

Reptan and Crocod stopped facing each other for a few seconds and turned to face Liz. Even with Liz's head raised, Reptan and Crocod did not notice Lee sitting on Liz's back. Liz began to talk to the two, using general conversation to break the ice and get more information about what triggered this dispute. She continued talking to the two bearded dragons as if she could have been their mother, sister, or long-lost best friend. She did so professionally and calmly, but she was not judgmental. They both listened without interrupting, and this went on for several minutes. Liz, Reptan, and Crocod talked about everything, from the weather and entertainment to sports and her everyday family life. Although Liz did all of the talking, as she spoke, Reptan and Crocod listened and nodded in agreement.

When Liz, Reptan, and Crocod were finished talking, it was as if they had known each other forever, as if it were indeed a reunification of some long-lost friends. They smiled at each other as if Liz had given them a gentle rebuke but with a smile. She urged them to stop fighting. The three of them stood there, Liz with Reptan and Crocod together, carrying on their casual conversation, and during all this time, none of the conversations involved Lee.

It was not a very long conversation, but one topic led to another, and these topics eventually led back to what they had just witnessed: all the destruction caused by Oscar. Once Liz could get all their differences out of the way, the conversation turned to discussions about the ants and how much she looked forward to helping them.

Reptan and Crocod paused for a second, smiled, and looked at each other; Reptan said, "I saw her first," but he was interrupted by Crocod answering, "No, *I* saw her first."

This brief exchange, done in a whisper, was meant for something other than Liz to hear, but Liz could quickly put two and two together. Liz got hints from Reptan and Crocod that they did not want to discuss the ants. Instead, Liz thought the two of them tried to get back to acting as they did when they were both at war. Their words playfully turned their questioning to her. Questions such as how she liked the neighborhood, what she thought of Oscar's newfound toy, etc.

Reptan and Crocod followed up with another series of questions. It was a process in which one lizard would ask Liz a question, then the other would look at him with a cross eye, and then the other would ask a follow-up question, going back and forth. Liz soon realized they wanted to fight each other because they either admired or liked her, which was how they tried to get her attention. This was how both male lizards behaved when fighting for dominance when trying to win over a mate. A blunt next question from Liz confirmed her suspicion, when she asked if they were in conflict over territory as regards to her, and they both answered yes.

Liz told them she was very flattered, but they should not be competing for something neither could get, and this rivalry needed to end at once. She said this with a stern voice and without a smile this time.

Reptan and Crocod had always admired Liz for her courage and bravery and for being beautiful and graceful. Reptan lived primarily in the tree in Oscar's yard, while Crocod spent most of his time living in the grass on the ground. Because Liz traveled on the ground and sometimes up in the tree, she had passed by many male lizards, including these two, without necessarily speaking to or acknowledging either one at any time.

They knew she was not afraid to try and do new things, go to new places, and meet new people, and the icing on the cake was that she was also very kind and compassionate. They both knew Liz was one of the friendliest of all the lizards around, which made her the most desirable of the lizards if looking for a mate, both on the ground and in the trees.

Although she didn't have to, Liz thought she needed to chat with them briefly. She went into an explanation, complete with tears, about the destruction of the ants she and Lee had just witnessed. Reptan and Crocod sympathized and asked Liz if she could see them joining forces to help the ants in any way or if there was a way to have the three of them work together to accomplish a unified goal or common cause. Liz smiled, knowing that the whole tears performance had worked (though her tears were real.) Reptan and Crocod stood before Liz, deciding to join her in helping the ants rebuild their once-proud home, which was now in their shared best interest. In each of their minds, it was a chance for them to compete on something in front of Liz, something she would be interested in sticking around to watch until the end, and perhaps allow each of them to become Liz's mate.

Liz then tilted her head slightly so they could see Lee on her back. Still, this time, it was not an aggressive stare, but for Liz, it was more of showing Repton and Crocod that *Hey, look who I have with me as a friend* kind of stare. At first, Lee, Reptan, and Crocod just stared back at each other, then at Lee.

Lee tried hard to hide any tears that may have formed as a result of the tremendous loss he had just suffered, but at the same time, Lee did not want to show any weakness. Even though he did not have the strength to face other ants or lizards, he hid those emotions well.

Liz told Lee he could now get down off her back. As there was nothing to fear, Lee was hesitant at first, with Reptan and Crocod still standing right there, but after a second or two, he slowly did what Liz asked and began to climb down while keeping his eyes planted firmly on Reptan and Crocod. Both lizards looked at Lee, and their eyes followed him down. Liz stared fearlessly at Reptan and Crocod as if to tell them, this *is my friend; he will not be harmed.* Lee slowly reached the ground and stood beside Liz's front legs.

At first, Reptan and Crocod were motionless as they stood silently in front of Liz and now Lee. Both were still filled with that adrenalin built up from when they were about to confront each other. And they both still had that competitive spirit of wanting to get Liz's attention and, at the same time, perhaps wanted to eat Lee. That sugar rush running through their veins from eating some of the dead ants earlier had since worn off; maybe they now had the hidden desire to eat one more ant, and Lee was definitely on the menu. Being aware that they could not eat Lee with Liz standing there, they had since calmed down from what they thought was their macho competition, thinking they knew what Liz wanted. They knew they were wrong about Liz and now had definite proof that Liz was unlike any other female lizard they had ever encountered.

They quickly concluded that hostile competition was what the other female lizards would have wanted, not Liz. Now that they will be working with Liz, they had better not let her down or appear not to do as she wanted. Going from fighting for Liz's attention to helping her with the ants would be a stretch. Still, with Liz's friendship and guidance guaranteed, or at least her admiration as the ultimate prize, this was a challenge they both would gladly accept. As a bonus, one of them might look better than the other to Liz.

Reptan and Crocod walked off together. They agreed not to fight but would compete on the playing field if needed and not on the battlefield. Both were still skeptical about whether they could trust the ants or whether the ants would trust them, as lizards tend to eat ants. However, with Liz present and offering guidance, they thought, what could go wrong?

Liz's conversation convinced Reptan and Crocod to leave it up to her to gain the rest of the ants' trust. She, Reptan, and Crocod decided to return to where the mound was. Liz wanted to show them what remained of the ants that were burnt and crushed by Oscar. Reptan and Crocod had to cover their noses when they got to the site. The smell of burnt flesh from the gas was everywhere. Reptan and Crocod shook their heads in disbelief at the magnitude of the destruction in the areas they had not seen before. Whether they were faking it or not, Liz and Lee were convinced.

Reptan and Crocod did not eat any more of the remaining deceased ants, and they kept quiet, folding their palms in front of them as if to pray. Lee, with his head down, appeared depressed and completely stressed out. Walking with Reptan and Crocod back to where the mound was, they paused and formed a circle, holding hands as if to have a moment of silence.

After that brief silence, Lee was in front of Liz, still between her front legs. Liz did not walk fast ahead of him but rather at a steady pace that would allow him to keep up while providing shade for him as they were both visually surveying the damage.

There was now a sense of calm in Lee's mind; for the first time, he was not scared of any of the lizards he had just met for the first time. Along the way, every once in a while, all four would stop here and there, saddened by the look at death's path of destruction. Lee started to shake his head with his hands on his hips. Liz told Lee she sympathized with his loss but promised that all three of them, Reptan, Crocod, and herself, would help. Reptan and Crocod looked at each other and nodded in agreement; neither one was about to defy or appear to disagree with Liz.

Lee's thoughts continued to himself, but these were thoughts of ways to get back at Oscar for destroying his home. He thought that in addition to helping rebuild the mound, he would wait until Liz was out of earshot, and that way, he might be able to talk with Reptan and Crocod, whom he now considered his new friends. He was sincerely convinced that all the lizards could help him, and the other ants get even with Oscar somehow.

Liz approached Lee and said with a wink, "What are you thinking? I can read your thoughts you know, and I know when something is bothering you."

Lee placed one of his hands on his chin and replied, "I just wish there was some way we could get back at Oscar for this tragedy."

Liz smiled at Lee and said, "My dear friend, I know you're upset, but no words of compassion can bring back the loss you have just suffered. Thinking about how to get back at Oscar will only cause you to have more headaches and heartache. She reminded him of the ancient proverb she had heard long ago, which had always stood with her. She said, "When you seek revenge, you must first dig two graves." Still looking at Lee, Reptan, and Crocod, who stood by listening, as Liz talked, she would use her hands, open them up wide, and raise them into the air for emphasis.

"Have we not seen enough death, pain, and destruction for one day or a lifetime?" asked Liz. "Let us concentrate on giving each other and all who need it a helping hand right now instead of trying to find ways to get back at those that we think have hurt us or have done us wrong in some way."

Reptan and Crocod looked at Liz, then at each other, and nodded in agreement. Lee continued to explain, this time turning his entire body to Reptan and Crocod and telling them with his hands open, palms facing up, that he had been through this type of destruction before. This kind of ruthless destruction was always unprovoked. He told them that unless something is done soon to these perpetrators, this type of activity will continue over and over and on and on indefinitely.

A tear slid down one side of his face, with Reptan and Crocod still looking on. Liz just listened to Lee and shed a tear in solidarity while he told his story. Lee told Reptan and Crocod of the great memories he had on the mound when he was a kid, the beauty of the neighborhood, and the unforgettable once-in-a-lifetime friends he made along the way. These memories were the first real memories he could recall while growing up.

He said, "I can still remember it as if it happened yesterday. Sadly, it's like one day, we're all together and having fun and enjoying life together when, the next day, we wake up, and they are gone." Sobbing, Lee said, "I am no longer together with my family and friends, having had one devastating destruction after another." Lee continued and told of the beloved queen he lost in the first destruction from his recent memory, the one before Valerie, and all the great souvenirs that once hung on the walls of the mound. These included birthdays, anniversaries, and notable accomplishments—those memories that were now scattered, not just over that yard, but down the drain, displaced and torn into a million pieces.

Lee continued to explain that the destruction of mounds is like a hurricane. Just like hurricanes, they are always given names by the ants' queen; all the names of these destructions are male names, and once that mound is destroyed, those names are retired forever.

Lee also told Reptan and Crocod about this one time he vividly could recall when he first moved into one of the new mounds with his family.

He said, "There were three of us, and I was the eldest." Lee said life was simpler back then, as he did not have to stress and worry about anything. Growing up, he never understood the whole thing about being the breadwinner or the designated leader. "I think anyone can be the leader or the breadwinner, voluntarily or involuntarily. We all have it in us to lead somehow, but it has not yet come to the surface for some. I don't understand or agree with the statement that by being the oldest, I should lead or set an example for others to follow. We all have our unique definition of what success, failure, and happiness should look like." Lee continued, "We should all have our own rules, preferences, likes and dislikes, which we should use to drive our ambition."

Lee was briefly interrupted by applause from Reptan, Crocod, and Liz, who said, "Amen, my brother, amen."

"I still can recall the first time my parents went out and brought back food for me and my brothers," Lee continued. "This was a particularly memorable feast, although all feasts are in some way. Invitations were sent to all the mounds whenever there was a feast in our colony. There was always a variety of food to choose from, including different breads, chicken, and fruits, with enough to go around and plenty of leftovers, enough to last for today and tomorrow. Every feast was like a Thanksgiving feast. We were always very thankful for our above-average abundance of food, but most importantly, for the time spent with many friends and family nearby. Back then, we all thought the mound we lived in was a very secure home, even though we lived near the water. I was young, and being at home with Mom and Dad was one of the most joyous things one could ever remember.

"In high school, I remember a competition among several schools and prominent families to design a new mound. There were many entries. The designs range from ultra-modern to old-fashioned, flat, and tall. The one we created was flat, laid in the grass, and designed with some leaves covering overhead to protect it from rain. As luck would have it, we designed the winning mound. The queen of the day invited the entire mound to a grand ball for a prize. Even the ones who did not win were invited, and my family was supposed to be the guest of honor at this feast at the queen's dwelling. It turned out to be one grand celebration. Indeed, it is one which, up to this day, I've always remembered. This was reminiscent of the evening Oscar planted the 'red food,' which the ants and lizards gathered to watch and share. It was also supposed to celebrate the past year's good fortune and the queen's royal jubilee. But unlike how Oscar's feast turned out, our feast was for the good of all involved."

Fortunately for Lee, he was not feeling well on the day he put a feast together. As a result, his parents joined him as he stayed home that day. On that day, Lee said he thought gathering the food was too easy. Some of the ants thought it was odd for food that looked so good, so eye-catching, and appealing to the eyes and nose. Lee thought the food was just too good to be thrown out.

Lee could not have imagined that this food would turn out to be his friends' and relatives' last supper. It was a day that most of them thought would be just another beautiful and uneventful day. But it was this occasion, on that one fateful day, where one minute you are with your friends, family, and loved ones, and the next, you do not get a chance to say the things you were thinking. From that day on, Lee learned that we could never wait for the perfect time, as there is no such time as the right moment.

"The things and the people you wanted to forgive and forget, the people to whom you've always wanted to say something, the things you have always wanted to apologize for . . . The ones you wanted to say, 'I love you,' the ones you wanted to let know that you're sorry for something you did a few weeks, months, or even years ago. Those are the things that cannot and must never wait," said Lee.

That was the first time Lee said he remembered that more than 90% of his mound, almost its *entire* population, was eliminated in a single event! It was the first record Lee had of such a massive loss and the first time growing up that he could recall loving so much, being so close to so many, and losing so many in the same short time. He knew these ants growing up through elementary, junior, and high school. It is one of his first memories of hearing about or learning about Oscar, the homeowner who supplied all the food, laid it out, and made it easy for the ants to take. By the time Lee got to say the words "high school" to Reptan, Crocod, and Liz, he was interrupted, and his terrible sobbing wound down as another ant came walking by.

It was Cindee who stopped in front of Lee. Cindee was similar in many ways to Liz as a fire ant. Cindee, like Liz, was also brilliant, extremely athletic, and exceptionally clever among the fire ants in her colony. Cindee had a unique way of expressing her beauty and confidence. For her, it would be doing so in a way that challenged the competitive spirit of both males and females in the colony, challenging them to match or duplicate her many actions and achievements. She could demonstrate her talents at times without even uttering a single word.

Regarding the events when ants compete, the competition is more about gathering and killing for food, even if it means attacking an enemy colony and taking their food and their favored relaxing place. But in Cindee's case, more than anything else, her definition of competition was always for the same result—she only wanted to be the queen. So, whatever the competition or dispute she got into, displaying leadership qualities as a way to become a queen was always the end game. If Cindee were ever to get into a fight, this would not necessarily be a physical fight, but if it were, it would be like any other ant fight—a fight to the death.

Usually, in an ant fight, whichever side loses, the winning side will take the other side's eggs for themselves as their own. Once these eggs are hatched, the new ants become slaves of their conquerors and are forced to obey their new masters in the new colony.

Lee and some other ants within the mound knew of Cindee and all she stood for. Seeing her vividly display her intentions from a long time ago, Lee realized she was evidently pursuing the throne, and her calculation seems to have intensified since the last extermination. Cindee did not keep her obvious desires secret; nevertheless, by her brave actions and bossy attitude, everyone knew anyway. She would confidently walk past the likes of Liz, Reptan, and Crocod without a blink and looked them up and down as she walked past with neither a smile nor a frown, all with no hint of fear in her steps.

Today, as she walked, she stopped and stood directly before Lee, facing him forehead-to-forehead. Lee didn't have to look to see or hear her coming. Ants don't have ears to hear; they hear through the vibrations that come up through their feet from the ground. They also have eyes and two antennas on their forehead to identify their mates and warn them of incoming enemies.

Cindee knew Lee, and Lee knew of her, and not just through the legendary reputation that preceded her. Thinking back, they both went to the same middle and high school. In high school, she was the only female on some men's teams, playing basketball and softball with the guys. On several occasions, Cindee was also a fill-in for the other traditionally male-dominated sports. In college, Cindee was once head of both the debate and drama clubs. These two positions would serve her well later in life, as she could be dramatic when arguing with someone. Her aggressive nature had earned her the nickname, "The Iron Ant." All the other male and female ants tended not to challenge or approach her under any circumstance as they feared she would not make them look good in the eyes of their peers, including the male workers who would never come to her to ask her to go out on a date.

In social settings outside of her home, whether she was somewhere standing by herself or even in the presence of her parents, especially her father, approaching her was not for the timid. In her father's eyes, no one in their colony, or their mound, for that matter, was ever good enough for his little princess. Her father treated her so much like royalty that even the dreaded Red fire ants that occasionally would encounter her would maintain some distance after first making any eye contact. Her confidence even prevented the elders from questioning her or publicly criticizing her. The elders and everyone else in her colony knew that she had set the bar so high that no one could attain the standard she projected and commanded.

Some, though, mainly the older male ants, thought she came across as being too masculine, too competitive, and a tomboy. Those attributes are primarily the reason that made all males avoid her. Most of her opponents and supporters would agree that, in conversation, she was just too blunt and direct for sensitive issues. Cindee could not sugarcoat lousy news as well as her fellow ants did, and this lack of sensitivity made her less favorable to be queen. Also, it may be especially unlikely for her to find a mate.

Despite being at the top of her classes and by far the most admired in every field she competed in, luck was not on her side in the elections as it was when she was in school. She was voted down twice for the top spot of the monarchy, but that did not deter her pursuit. Giving orders randomly to those she thought were not doing their job meant, at times, she was refuted by some in the colony, but this did not stop her from pursuing leadership. In her last two election attempts, she failed to gather enough votes for the crown, and those losses were by a wide margin. Still, in the last election, the poll numbers were narrower than in previous years. This was helped in part by a large number of female workers who turned out for the election. Still, it was widely believed that most—if not all—men did not want this one woman—let alone such a strong woman—in charge, so they voted against her en masse.

Cindee neither trusted nor feared the lizards, and she would sometimes say things in front of the other ants and, at times, the lizards, which provoked them to rattle their cages. In her politics, Cindee was a typical example of some of today's politicians. If she were to step into the spotlight, this would be an opportunity to turn every event into a campaign stop and make a speech. She would preach and, just like politicians, spread bad news about her opponents and enemies, so lizards, frogs, and other ants were all fair game. The main target of her attacks was the current queen.

Cindee once told the lizards, "You are not apes, and we are not Tarzan." She had reasons to doubt the friendship of the lizards, but they were reasons she never shared with everyone else. She would use every opportunity to continue stoking fear and hate in the ants' minds whenever given the chance. For Cindee, this mentality included the lizards and other creatures that would feed on ants. She would also criticize the current queen for not protecting the colonies adequately.

Although she knew of Liz's friendship with Lee, she still did not trust the lizards when it came to the relationship with other non-ant species . One of Cindee's most famous reasons, and by far her most prominent rallying call for unity in the mistrust of the lizards, was that she saw most of these lizards as nothing more than enemies of the ants and felt they were not to be trusted.

Cindee also thought they could not be kept or raised as pets, guardians, or friends. If the lizards ever found themselves where no one was looking, they would not pass up the opportunity to eat one or all of the ants, even the ones they once called their friends. Cindee said the lizards go out of their way to earn your trust by highlighting matters the ants feared most and offering to fix these issues. Still, these lizards would never provide a specific map for accomplishing this fix. Cindee said that all the lizards would offer some broad, drawn-out ideas without specifics, just like the politicians.

However, she never convinced Lee, any other lizards, or a select few ants of her point of view. Still, these very vocal points of view always got her the attention she craved. In most of her public appearance speeches, she used fear, particularly fear of the unknown, when talking to the elders, knowing they would take everything she said back to their mounds and preach it like it was the gospel. One of Cindee's most vocal attacks on the current queen was telling the ants that Valerie could not protect the colonies from outside threats. She would say that protecting the borders and population of each colony should be the most critical job of any queen, and if she, Cindee, were queen, it would be paramount.

This was one of the surest ways to get the ants to listen and see her viewpoint. This was to instill in them the idea that she had the confidence and the vision to lead them.

There was a time when Cindy could be considered kinder and gentler, but that was a long time ago when she was younger. Cindee had always had to learn how to be tough growing up. Although her father had spoiled her before he passed, she had been an only child whose parents died when she was at an early age. So, she had to learn survival skills, care for herself, and trust herself and her instincts.

Rex was the most similar to Cindee on the lizard's side. Everyone knew him and considered him to be Cindee's male counterpart. If Rex and Cindee were of the same species, they would make up the perfect couple. Like Cindee, his path, too, was fearful to cross, at least in how he presented himself to other lizards. Rex considered the other lizards to be more vulnerable creatures than the ants, whom he knew outnumbered the lizards several times over.

No one was ever sure how he got the name Rex, whether it was given at birth or something he assumed. Maybe Rex was just for his initials, or it may have been a pseudonym he picked up along the way. Maybe it was a nickname he gave himself because he believed that he resembled a tyrannosaurus-rex due to his congenital disability that left him with tiny front feet.

Rex once said he saw himself as a true descendant of the dinosaurs, although most scholarly elders in the lizard world that roamed the yard often would dismiss this as rubbish. They would tell him he was descended from a snake, perhaps as a jab at his personality. Unfortunately, for all of his critics, Rex had thick skin, and he would disregard any of their criticisms or comments without a second thought.

Quite often, he tended to stand on his back two legs, fold his two front legs, and extend his dewlap many times. He would do it, especially in the presence of another male lizard, as a show of dominance. Unlike the other lizards in the yard, he did this whether or not he felt threatened or had something to say.

He was shorter than most—if not all—the other adult lizards roaming about this yard, so to compensate for his height and size, standing on his back legs was his way of showing off his stamina. It made him appear taller and more intimidating. Like Cindee, he did not trust most of the other creatures that did not look like him, not only the ants but some of the lizards, frogs, and birds. But unlike Cindee, he wasn't competing for any political position or status upgrade other than the attention he loved. His view of the ants was that he saw them as nothing more than food. But he did have some respect for them because of their vast numbers.

Liz was the only lizard he somewhat trusted, and he selected others like ER. However, he did not depend too much on others like Liz did. Perhaps it was because of her beauty and overwhelmingly friendly personality, or because she was so popular and fearless, just like him, albeit for different reasons. Hearing Cindee talk about her outlook on how bad matters were and how much better she could make their lives, he saw a version of himself in her despite coming from a different species.

Regardless of his often negative comments and his carrying on about everything, many other lizards and ants didn't immediately rush out to hear anything he had to say. The only lizards who would come out to listen to him and speak at times were the ones who happened to be walking by and happened to hear him talking. There were also the ones who needed a reason to get out of the house, and they would gather while standing in no formation but more of a cluster mess while listening to him. These would be only lizards, seldom any ants, who would just be going about their daily business, crossing each other's paths.

Those very few ants seen standing around anywhere close by were just the ones who managed to escape the disaster and wanted a mental escape in light entertainment. Since these ants did not want to be at home suffering from another day of cabin fever, Rex, and Cindee were often on the speakers' corner of the day. Most ants and lizards did not want to sit at home listening to the radio daily, at least in what was left of their so-called home.

Listening to a speech from Rex or Cindee always provided that escape, that entertainment. Altogether, no more than a dozen lizards would gather at any given time to listen to Rex, that was enough to offer him an audience too often listening to his nonsense. Cindee and Rex were two of a kind, both loved and craved attention, although for different reasons.

Across from the lizards and where Rex was standing, Cindee was once again trying to be the focus of attention. This time, it was by dressing up in some obscure outfit and speaking even louder. She had this object in her hair that resembled a painted mohawk, and it appeared that it was part of her skull. She wore a bright red T-shirt that said, "Make the colonies great again." Whatever reaction she could get or was trying to convey was working . Dozens and dozens of ants were standing around. As usual, she just gave her opinion, which was not called for in the situation. This time, they had to address limited food supplies. Worst of all, Cindee was now armed with a bullhorn in one of her hands and a raised fist in the other.

Despite most of them still shaken from the last disaster, she called out for all the remaining ants to come together and hear her pep talk of sorts, and she made it clear that lizards were not invited. Cindee felt the ants didn't need lizards to come out and work the area, competing for the same scraps while the crowd consisted of all the remaining living ants. Some of the lizards were across from the ants, where Rex stood. They were joining their friends and family, who had been severely injured, some hopping around with broken limbs; some of these ants even had systematic difficulties seeing and hearing.

On the other hand, the lizards were leaping and jumping around and landing on whatever seemed to move—eating away at anything resembling food and drink in whatever spot.

In her speech, Cindee told the ants they must organize, rebuild their mound, and make the colonies great again. She told them they could all accomplish this by relying on themselves and working together. These sentences were the same things that the queen would sometimes say to rally her troops, and as she said it, she would receive lots of cheering, giving her a standing ovation each time. She would continue her speech, saying something else while raising a fist.

While Cindee seemed to have all the momentum and attention on her side, she quickly took a dark turn. What's the old saying, absolute power corrupting absolutely? She told the ants they must also gather this strength and courage to march into Oscar's home and eat through his furniture and food.

"This will send a message to Oscar that we're here in his home and we are not leaving," she said confidently.

She continued her rant, knowing full well that Oscar would only get upset, and this would make him want to attack them. She insisted that they could get out of his way immediately after they were spotted, and they could then retaliate by attacking him, biting him and his family to the point where they must go to the hospital.

By now, these speeches had commanded everyone's attention, even when discussing issues that were not universally appealing or would not apply to everyone. But what held their attention was the talk about something everyone could relate to, they had to think about stopping the attacks from Oscar and protecting their homes.

Cindee spoke with fire in her voice, and as she did, it seemed her nostrils would expand with each new word, and nothing but flares would be released in every sentence. She continued to raise her fist in the air with each sentence. Several times during her speech, with her hands constantly in the air, she intentionally turned away from the ants and stared the lizards in the face.

Her speech went on for several minutes, and for every one of those minutes, she appeared to be angrier than the last. Whether among themselves or towards anyone within earshot of her speech, no one, especially the other ants, booed or said a word of displeasure to her or about her. Doing nothing made it feel like she had their backing; at least, that's the vibe she was getting from the crowd during her rant. Peer pressure caused them to want to stand there and listen to her without interrupting or expressing a single objection.

During all this, Liz, Reptan, and Crocod would look at each other, then back at Cindee without commenting, not shaking their heads so much; even Rex had nothing to say.

Following Cindee's speech, Rex came walking by. He was accompanied by some red fire ants, holding placards. As Rex approached Cindee, she could see the placards reading, "Protect our borders," and "Queen V, time to step down." Rex stopped, but the ants walked past a smiling Cindee. Rex was the only lizard out there who did not go out of his way to act as a peacemaker like Liz. Nor did he pretend to be friendly or polite. Perhaps secretly, he did not think Liz was all that, but if he did, he would never make those feelings public. Besides his discomfort, he knew deep down that most of the other lizards who liked Liz did not think much of him. He didn't like being around any of them, for that matter, and he did not give much thought to what they thought of him. He would never appear to be angry with Liz, at least not in public; he primarily disliked the fact that she would associate herself with the likes of the ants, and that was something he could never understand.

Lying flat on his stomach and crawling forward, Rex approached Liz; he raised his head up and down with a brief pause each time. He turned and looked at Cindee across the way, then turned back to face Liz and asked, "Why would you associate herself with these hateful creatures?"

Liz twisted her head to one side as if she was about to answer his question, but she did not speak.

Rex, still staring at her, asked, "Hmmmm?"

Liz said, "I was surprised at you, that you did not immediately go over and attack the ants right away, mainly Cindee, after listening to what she had to say. Was it because Reptan and Crocod were standing close by? Was it the thought that Reptan and Crocod were so close to the ants, and you thought causing a scene in front of them would place you on the wrong side of all our lizards?" Liz smiled. "Come to think of it, you did not even try to make eye contact with Reptan and Crocod," said Liz.

Both Rex and Liz fell silent, and Liz waited for Rex to say something. Liz did not want to feel as if she would have to continue to smile at him while waiting for him to reply. Liz refused to acknowledge Rex as having any influence. So, when he first approached her with his question, in her mind, she thought that he would always come to her with a friendly or sometimes sarcastic hello or good morning, so she stood silent . Liz was not fearful of Rex. And it was not because of Reptan and Crocod, who always stood nearby. Not that she would need the assistance of Reptan and Crocod to help her defend herself against the likes of Rex. She could easily stand her ground against Rex, even if he were verbally aggressive. Liz's scheme showed Rex that she was not intimidated by him.

She looked at him directly and, raising her head slightly above his, said, "If you have an issue with me, you should take it up with me directly, not with the ants or other lizards."

With Liz standing this close to him and Reptan and Crocod standing in his presence as well, Rex saw an opportunity to do what he thought would be a great chance to embarrass Liz but without appearing to threaten her. His goal was to teach her a lesson for keeping the likes of Lee as a friend.

Rex stood in front of all the ants and lizards, and by them staring back at him, he thought that he now had their full attention, if only for a moment. He slowly rose from his stomach, tilted his head, and faced Liz in the pose that lizards use when they are about to challenge each other to a fight. With a smirk, knowing fully that Liz would not want to turn down any challenge from a male or female, he said to her, "I challenge you to a duel."

Liz's smiling response without hesitation was, "I gladly accept." Liz then asked what the prize was and what this duel would consist of.

Rex continued, saying, "We will have rules, and you two, pointing at Reptan and Crocod, can be the judges for the competition as we go along."

Liz, Reptan, and Crocod did not immediately comment, and they stood silent to hear what else Rex had to say about this duel. Rex began to lay out his plan, this time in more detail. Reptan and Crocod glanced at each other, then looked at Rex and smiled, shaking their heads but not necessarily in agreement with him, more or less just acknowledging what was just said.

The fact that Rex was going up against Liz in a challenge meant this would be a box-office sellout. Challenging her to any contest would draw the attention of everyone, not just the lizards but also the ants and frogs and all the other creatures that call this yard their home. Liz opened her mouth as if she were about to speak, and everyone suddenly got quiet, which was a common occurrence when she'd speak, but they soon saw she was yawning. Rex took it as an insult and a way for Liz to tell him she was bored with his plan, but he let her have her moment.

Word of Liz and Rex's challenge quickly spread around the yard, and when Cindee heard from ER about Rex's challenge to Liz, the contest gave her a great idea of to show off her skills, whatever they were.

She put down her bullhorn and immediately walked over to Lee, stood before his face, and said, "Since you seemed so friendly with the lizards…"

But she was abruptly interrupted before finishing what she was about to say. Lee, who did not want to hear what she had to say, turned his head, flashing the palm of his hand to her face as he walked away.

A unanimous "Ooh" came from Reptan and Crocod, as well as a few ants. This was a blatant slap in the face to Cindee, who picked up the bullhorn and placed it before her mouth.

She yelled, "I, challenge you, Lee, to the same contest as Rex and Liz."

Lee paused. He seemed puzzled, and there was a hush from Crocod, Reptan, and the other ants.

Lee then walked back, approached Cindee, and asked her, "Are you stupid or crazy? How can we get involved in the same contest as Liz and Rex? After all, they are lizards, and we are not only of different sizes and capacities but also of different species. The lizards are bigger, stronger, and faster than we are," Lee continued.

Cindee responded, "But we're ants, and as ants, we are blessed with the ability to lift twenty times our body weight."

Lee did not want to appear weak, and turned down the challenge, at least in front of the other Lizards and ants. So, he paused, then walked up to Cindee and asked her to explain the rules of this challenge and how it would be carried out before he would agree to it.

She put down the bullhorn and said, "Yes, let me explain."

The contest, as Cindee explained, would involve stunts that would determine, among other things, who was fast and brave enough to get out from under a foot as it was coming down, which was code for Oscar's foot. Then, they would move on to climbing a tree in the black forest. The black forest was the shaded and darkest part of the yard. This would be followed by walking and running across an open field, another part of the yard. This well-known area, everyone knew, could harbor a lot of creatures that prey on ants. It is an area well known for birds such as hawks, owls, eagles, all the birds of prey that hunt and eat ants, and lizards. According to Cindee, this is where they would assemble. It had earned the nickname "Death Path."

This was also the path that Oscar would take for his daily walks whenever he was walking back and forth in his backyard and sometimes playing with Blondi. Oscar would walk with his hands in his pocket, staring at the ground here and there as if thinking to himself while walking, and he would be stepping on anything he encountered that moved. Anything not fast enough to get out from under his foot would not live to see the light of another day. Lee seemed content with the rules and what was involved. He smiled and told Cindee that he agreed and would accept. Cindee was pleased as she gave Lee a wide smile.

After several discussions going back and forth about the proposed rivaling duels, it came down to a general agreement that the contest would take place the following day, at high noon. The ants and lizards agreed that their contest would occur back-to-back, with the first competition being that of the lizards, Liz, and Rex. ER was entrusted to get the word out about not just the lizard's duel but the ant's challenge as well.

The small crowd gathered, listened to both challenges, and began to mumble among themselves; some even started placing bets. After a while and much discussion, the crowd slowly began to disperse.

The most terrible things in life always seem to happen when we are most vulnerable, usually when it's dark and we are exposed to the unexpected. Sometimes, though, the unexpected could be a good thing. The old saying goes, "What does not kill you makes you stronger."

Throughout the night, Liz would get up from her usual sleep cycle for a few minutes or so here and there. Throughout the night, she thought about the rules, who and how many would show up, and where the contest would take place. She also considered how Reptan and Crocod would judge the contest and whether it would be done fairly. Other than having those racing thoughts, it was an otherwise peaceful night, although, to Liz, the night felt long.

Everyone could agree that today was at least a very long day, and now that it was night, they were all a bit tired. The ants had had enough of seeing what had happened to the mound and their family. It was also challenging to see that it had come down to Cindee, Lee, and the others wanting to go on with even more infighting.

Most of the ants thought this challenge was more about Cindee and Lee trying to prove who was better. Still, with Rex in the mix, it came down to those who always wanted to be a leader or at least have the most influence. The elder lizards felt the same way after bearing witness earlier to Reptan and Crocod during their disagreements.

As far as Liz was concerned, she did not care what the others thought; she did not have that much love or admiration for Rex and wanted to use this opportunity to put him in his place, hopefully, once and for all. She also enjoyed the talk of the upcoming challenge to be held the next day. But she hoped it would soon be over so she could finally go to bed and rest for what would become another long, adventurous day ahead. Between the ants and lizards, other than those wary thoughts, it was also a very peaceful night. Lee did spend the night very close to Liz. She comforted him throughout the night, which seemed to keep them both calm, making for a restful night.

The next day was bright and sunny. By now, most of the corpses of the deceased ants from the previous day had been eaten overnight by various scavengers; not even so much as the bones remained. Also, the smell of all the fuel poured onto them was gone, and what remained of the dead now were mainly small pieces of skeletons. Marks in the ground identified where the deceased once lay.

What was left of the dead lizards was also eaten up by various scavengers, including ants, worms, and other lizards. There was not much in the sense of memories or mementos from the mound for the ants to view, recall, or even think about. Knowing what they knew took place in the days prior, the remaining ants had no home to go to, and there wasn't even much food—today had to be a much better day, regardless of the outcome. Today, by all means, indeed had to be a better day than yesterday because, unlike other kinds of challenges, this was not a challenge to the death or to become queen or any other leader; this contest was viewed by most as a grudge match.

Lee and Liz got up well-rested in the morning from what eventually became a good night's sleep for their respective contests. Liz put together a light breakfast for Lee, a granola bar and orange juice. On the other hand, Liz tended not to eat that much, if anything, or at least not that early in the morning; a drink of room-temperature water would do it for her. She wanted to ensure Lee had plenty to eat, providing the energy he needed for his duel. Not a feast, as if it was his last meal, but more a feast to give him the stamina she thought he would need to put in a good fight.

Liz, the more seasoned hunter, could adapt quickly to any environment and situation. Since her opinion and advice carried so much weight, she assured Lee, with a commitment and a pat on his back, that no matter what happened today, she would still honor her word and help him and his family to rebuild their mound, no matter the time frame and the material involved. On the other hand, Lee reassured Liz that no matter the outcome, he would always be her friend.

It was now close to the time for the challenge, and spectators and challengers were assembled in the field that was Oscar's backyard, where the duel was to be held. It was a calm midday with no sign of Oscar or Penni anywhere in site, not even their dog Blondi.

Thanks to ER for getting the word out, primarily by having plenty of placards and flyers posted, inviting everyone to come out and not only watch the contests but also, for those who still need to do so, place bets on the outcome. The turnout was impressive. As far as everyone could hear and see, many spectators came to witness the contest. This location was turned into an open arena, the designated spot in Oscar's backyard, complete with seating and standing-room-only areas, customized and separated for lizards and ants alike. It was already agreed that Reptan and Crocod, the two lizards who were previously going to fight over Liz, would be the judges for the Liz and Rex contest. Liz had some relief from any anxiety she was feeling, but she was not expecting any special favors.

As for the ants, two random ants stepped up to be judges, both of whom were female, and both, at one time or the other, were considering running for the position of queen. Both of these ants, however, later dropped out of the race to the crown after getting tired of constantly fighting a losing battle with Cindee in the form of arguments about customs and policies. Some of these battles were public and occurred inside and outside Cindee's social circle. They made a promise, a commitment to be fair—to Cindee— and in front of everyone else, especially the elders.

Just before the start, the crowds gathered and quickly formed a circle.

There were set patterns with ants on one or more sides and lizards on the other. They were all mixed in their seating and standing in assigned areas, which took place just before the contest began. Since it was already decided that the lizards would go first, it was agreed that this start would be done with a simple "on your mark, get set, and go" voice command from ER. The most straightforward instructions would come next, essentially retelling the rules discussed the previous day, and the contestants would follow a previously determined obstacle course. This course was primarily laid out and constructed by the ant workers and some of the leaf-cutter ants; very few lizards were involved in designing and placing materials.

This course included the usual muddy water, food chunks, and the occasional corpses of ants and lizards. These corpses were fake but laid out for maximum shock value and disorientation, a special request from Rex. Confident that she would be victorious, Liz appeared mentally ready for whatever the obstacle course held. Liz and Cindee were so satisfied that they did not participate in the ritual prayer or the national anthem before the contest began.

Even though Rex was firm and displayed his usual very aggressive macho nature, moving around as a boxer does just before a fight, Liz had the mentality of the home-court advantage, evident by her calm demeanor.

Lee was also confident of victory, not worried about trying to impress anyone; he did not care much about it. Cindee thought he would be too emotionally drained from the previous days to believe in himself or do anything too complicated; the least of these concerns was thinking of something that could go wrong or would happen to her. Cindee knew she had more to lose, although, to her, the monarchy's position was what was at stake.

In these events, where the outcome could go either way, there was always a sense of nervous anticipation, anxiety, and adrenaline affecting the participants and the spectators. The cheering for one side or the other proved that everyone had something to lose. This was true, especially for those who had bet money on the outcome.

The lizards lined up for both challenges, with about half cheering for Liz and the other half for Rex as the competition began.

When Rex and Liz started together and went through their respective obstacles, Rex smiled at the start, but that was perhaps just a show of overconfidence. If he was nervous, he didn't show it.

On the other hand, Cindee was off to a much quicker start than Lee. Maybe it was intentional, just common courtesy from Lee to let the woman take the lead, or as some had always thought, Cindee was just better at athletics.

The first challenge in the contest for both was the dreaded run across the yard. At first glance, with the lizards, it was a seamlessly easy thing to do. Still, as mentioned when the rules were explained to them, there would be twists and turns, unexpected obstacles that would challenge them, and potential accidents. These might show up anywhere along the way. As the lizards raced across the yard, they first encountered a deliveryman, bringing an online order to Oscar's house. For Oscar, all of his deliveries are made in the back to avoid porch pirates.

Even though he was walking on the paved part of the walkway leading up to Oscar's house, both lizards were able to avoid his feet, but this part was far from over. As the delivery man accidentally dropped the package on the grass, it rolled over a few times directly into the pathway where the lizards were running. The man quickly picked up the package, jumped a few steps, and placed it on the back porch. As he was leaving, he was running, and this time, Oscar's dog Blondi came out from behind him and was now chasing him. When he ran, he ran side to side in a zigzag manner across the lot, trying to dodge Blondi, who was following the same pattern. Both lizards kept changing course as they also ran, trying to avoid not just the delivery man's two feet but Blondi's four feet as well.

Liz easily won this leg of the first contest. Once she won, she did not boast or brag; she bowed and thanked everyone, then raised her fists once as she walked past, thanking everyone.

Lee also had challenges on the same path for the ants, minus the delivery guy. His obstacles included but were not limited to picking up food placed along the way and bringing it back to the makeshift, tastefully built mound for this contest. This proved extremely easy for him to win this leg against Cindee.

The second leg of Cindee and Lee's contest involved climbing a tree and digging a patch somewhere in that tree to bury some food for later. For this contest, Lee and Cindee had to make it easy for other ants to locate the food, not just now but several days later if needed, regardless of weather conditions like rain, sleet, or snow. To retrieve this food later, it would not be just Lee and/or Cindee who would need to be able to find it, but any other randomly selected ant in the mound should be able to find it later, and this had to be done without the help of an ant GPS.

Lee, like Liz, enjoyed this part of the challenge. Yet, unfortunately for Lee, Cindee won this segment of the contest. The entire race lasted no more than thirty minutes in Liz and Lee's contests, and they each had an army of cheerful fans on their respective sides.

Now, however, some new fire ants had moved into the area to witness the duel and look for a new place to call home. In addition to checking out where the old mound was located, it was as if they were tourists or new homeowners looking for an earthquake-free and hurricane-proof path to start a new life and build a new future. They came from far and near; some ants were arriving on the backs of snack wraps that flew by, and others on the trash blown along the way by the wind and on the backs of dried-up leaves.

This spot, chosen especially for the contest, showed that the cracks had been there for a while, as they looked like the same rock pattern from an old house, and the rocks and sand had little chance of being shifted. When the new fire ants in the area were walking around, they could see that there were visible signs where, once the water started flowing, it would now easily have an unobstructed path. Not only ants from other yards had come by, but lizards from other trees were also present, but these lizards were there to watch the contest.

In the end, Lee lost his contest to Cindee, but this does not seem to upset him or the other ants who vigorously support him. Many thought, including many of his supporters, that Cindee was much younger and had much more alethic ability, and she, by far, appeared to be the more intelligent of the two. Perhaps knowing that she had a lot more to lose than Lee meant she had put forth more effort. It was only apparent to one team, other than bragging rights, what the point of the victory was for either lizards or ants and what, by competing against these two precisely, the victor from each side would have accomplished. It was more about ego than anything else.

The win or loss seemed more like a victory for those who were not participating, particularly those placing bets, as it gave them a field day and the chance to socialize with both ants and lizards outside the comfort of their respective homes, even if it was just for part of one day.

With the challenge now long over, it was time to focus on the next big upcoming event. The ant's election of the new queen, which was to be held in one week, and this, being an election year, meant the campaign signs were up everywhere. That also meant that the candidates running against each other all selected ER to make their respective signs and attack ads for the other candidate. This also told ER they would make those signs according to each candidate's specifications.

The campaign ads were plastered over every avenue. These campaigns were all centered on tapping into the fear and mistrust of the different ant species. Although in everyday life, all of these candidates would appear civil and courteous in public and private, the discussions of the campaign's direction showed otherwise.

Lee, with the help of Liz, had the personal responsibility to plan and act quickly to recruit others and to execute those plans to rebuild the mound in the hope that rebuilding would bring all the ants back under one roof and one command, as this would have to be done once the new queen was selected. Lee and Liz thought they could do it in seven days or fewer. With some additional help from Cindee, Reptan, and Crocod, Lee hoped to get this all done, just among themselves.

Despite her victory and newfound fame, Cindee still held onto one of her favorite grudges for whatever reason. She was now focusing all her energy on the idea that Oscar should at least have to pay or feel some pain for the affliction he had consistently caused. In her opinion, he had consistently caused all the pain and suffering of the ants and lizards in and around his yard, and he needed to pay for it somehow.

Rex, who lost his contest with Liz, was now a disgruntled, bitter loser. He wanted to humiliate her by having her present and explain to the other lizards the purpose of her friendship with the ants. But this time, he wanted it done out in public. As if losing was not enough, he also wanted a rematch or another challenge for the chance to redeem himself, perhaps this time something more physical like a wrestling match.

His ego would not let him comprehend how a girl could have easily beaten him at something he thought he should have won. A rematch or another form of the challenge of his choosing would be ideal so he could show the other lizards that he was the intense, confident, macho leader they thought him to be and that he was the man to lead them into the future. Rex felt a sense of inferiority as Liz once again not only won the hearts and minds of her peers but also the respect of not just the lizards, but also the ants.

As part of his ongoing issue with Liz, Rex took a page from Cindee's playbook and now insisted that the lizards should retaliate against Oscar for using the blower and fuel on them. It seemed as though Cindee's influences were rubbing off on him, but few, other than Cindee herself on the ants' side, seemed to be interested in any Oscar talk.

After his duel, as Lee was walking back to where the makeshift mound was built, he came across a white trash bag that had stopped after having been blown in the wind. Lee was hungry and naturally curious; he thought some food might be inside the bag. Blown by the breeze, this bag got held up and stuck to the side of a trash can by a twig sticking out of a broken tree branch with the sharp edge pointing out. Lee cautiously walked around the bag first and then went inside it.

Once inside, he saw only a piece of paper with some prescription written on it. At first, he did not know what the prescription was for, as the name of the drug was an unpronounceable one. It seemed unlike the over-the-counter medication for headaches he had seen before. Still, the bottle displayed two or three scientific names, which were usually entirely different from the simple name used by the manufacturer for marketing.

Lee did not find food inside the bag, as he had hoped. Still, as he walked up to get a closer look at the prescription, just above where the name of the medicine was written, he saw it was a prescription for Oscar. Lee, at first, couldn't have been more impressed and intrigued. He began reading the description as to what the drug was to be used for, how often it was to be taken, and in what quantity. He saw it was an antihistamine. He knew the many medicines humans would take regarding stings and bites. He also knew that this meant Oscar had some ongoing allergies. Without these drugs, humans could or would have an allergic reaction to stings and bites, so this medication was no stranger to Lee.

Lee's heart rate accelerated. His eyes expanded to near capacity. He was excited and scared. Excited that if this information got into the wrong hands, it could be used for all kinds of nasty stuff and scared that he may have just stumbled upon the one way that Cindee and Rex had been talking about, the one way for everyone to get back at Oscar. It made him uneasy knowing he had this much power, making him uncomfortable having these evil thoughts. What if he had indeed stumbled upon this vital information that could harm Oscar's health? Then, the question arose: Should he bring this up with the other ants and perhaps even with the lizards? If left unchecked, this kind of information could—and most likely would—end up in the wrong hands and be used in unimaginable ways. Despite having reservations at first, Lee sat under the bag that gave him shade. This was a weight on his heart and mind, so now all he needed to do was get it off his chest.

Lee decided to take it back toward the mound to present it to Cindee and Liz. Still, he remained skeptical about what Cindee would do with it, perhaps show it to all the other ants. Lee mainly thought of the possible consequences and the response he might get from Liz. He was thinking that he would quickly come under fire from Liz, as she was now the presumed leader of the lizards, and she would be furious if it were not run by her first before presenting it to Cindee. Lee got up and walked out from under the shaded white bag. On his way to the mound, he approached where Liz stood alone, resting, and staring into the vast open yard.

He stood before her without saying a word and then presented her with his new finding. She looked at it and appeared puzzled, then reached out and accepted it. She opened it up and read it thoroughly. Liz read it, in its entirety, but silently to herself. She then looked down at Lee and asked him where he got it. Lee told her he found it next to the trashcan, pinned by a twig. He told Liz that he would mention this to Cindee as well, but Liz looked at Lee, and she appeared furious.

After reading it, she said in a stern tone, "This finding is not a game; it is not child's play either; it is more of a monumental discovery that could make the difference between life and death. It's a discovery that will require a well-thought-out response, not one that could provoke acting on the fly."

She looked over to the side, staring in the direction of Cindee and Rex conversing. No matter what Rex and the other lizards had to say, Liz's words, as the apparent new leader since the end of the challenge, now carried more weight, and she knew this.

For now, the details of the prescriptions remained solely in Liz's possession. She wanted to hold onto it while she and what she called her inner circle, meaning Reptan and Crocod, so that together, they could determine the most appropriate course of action. Liz said she wanted action, if any, based on a realistic and practical outcome. Liz approached Reptan and Crocod and asked them to play soothing music over the intercom. This was a way to get the lizards to loosen up, slow dance, and get comfortable with each other. This suggestion was her way to change the subject and making everyone think that everything was fine on the front lawn. Playing soft music was always a way to avoid suspicion, but for this occasion, it was also good for her to keep her mind off the new findings.

Liz said to Reptan and Crocod that she was hungry. In unison, they asked her what she would like to eat. She paused momentarily, realizing the food choices after this recent destruction of the area were limited. So, she immediately changed her mind and decided to go out and get something to eat and take the prescription letter with her.

She then ordered everyone, lizards, and remaining ants, to return home to be with their families and loved ones as Oscar seemed to have finished all the cleaning for the day. With that directive, the music suddenly stopped; for now, at least Liz, Reptan, and Crocod stood together. Liz held the prescription in her hands as she, Reptan, and Crocod watched as all the lizards and ants disbursed in various directions.

Once everyone left, Liz looked at Lee and noticed the expression of self-defeat and sorrow returning to his face. No words of comfort she could offer him could encourage him from the list of downer thoughts he was experiencing . First, he lost his home and his family and friends, and then he was beaten by a girl in a contest, and now, he felt guilty because he knew he had found the one thing he thought could hurt Oscar. All this weighed heavily on his mind. Each time he saw Cindee, those feelings would return. He felt disappointment from Liz that he thought Liz had shown him that she was unhappy because he had brought her this new information that held so much responsibility. But Lee tended to overthink things. This self-criticism he was doing could all be in his head.

He looked Liz in the eyes and said, "Thank you for all you have done for us so far."

Liz was silent, but she smiled back at him.

He held his head down and told her he wanted to return to where the mound once stood to reminisce. Liz seemed satisfied that she could be a good listener again and did not want Lee to go through the rest of the day reliving any more of his discomforts. He felt confident in showing and convincing her that the information he had just uncovered showed that even Oscar had some weaknesses. Maybe he even was beginning to have some compassion for Oscar, albeit very little, and he was worried about getting this information to Cindee because he now saw that Oscar also had this apparent weakness that was not previously known. Lee knew that the whole mound would understand once Cindee got this. Lee thought this weakness in the hands of the wrong people could lead to catastrophic thoughts and actions, so, for now, he was happy that it was in Liz's hands.

He began to walk with Liz in private to discuss this new set of information and the best course of action forward, if any. Together, they hoped they could devise a plan and convince the other ants and lizards that attacking the homeowner may or may not be the thing to do, at least not now. However, by keeping the information secret between Liz and him, Lee believed that he and Liz could at least discuss their options privately.

Liz still wanted to go and get something to eat and drink. As they walked together this time, Liz did all the listening. While walking, they approached Cindee. Despite some reservations at first, Lee, with Liz's blessing, decided they would stop to explain the information he had just found to Cindee, and tell her that he had already presented it to Liz. With the election fast approaching, Lee's thought process was that Cindee might become the new queen, and it would not be a good thing if she were not brought in on this information.

When Lee approached Cindee with Liz, Cindee, without waiting to hear him out entirely, turned her back and started to walk away, dismissing him. Lee knew right then that Cindee would not go along with the plan. Fresh off the victory from her duel, Cindee now had new friends who hung around her because of her newfound fame and increased strength. Cindee paused momentarily, stopped walking, and talking, and briefly turned around to listen to Lee. Still, she made it clear that she did not want to hear anything kind or offer sympathy to Oscar. She just wanted revenge, but Liz and Lee believed that maybe she wanted her voice recognized and her instructions followed.

This was Cindee's fifteen minutes of fame, and it seemed she intended to enjoy every second of her now, even more powerful, time in the spotlight. Cindee's only fear was that her time in the limelight was about to be dimmed by Liz and Lee's apparent weakness towards Oscar, as well as Liz's influence and new alliances. Cindee thought that with Liz and Lee's combined forces, they would be beyond her control and out of her influence if she did not act fast.

Cindee paused, turned around to Lee, and said, "This might be okay for you, and that is because you are soft-hearted and humble, but for me, I believe we should go all out and seek payback immediately."

Luckily for Lee, Cindee was talking to him now and not in front of the other ants. Liz stepped back so Lee and Cindee could converse privately. Lee felt confident that perhaps he could isolate her and have just the two of them sit down and talk so that he could reason with her and get her to see things his way, but only if she'd settle down and think about it. That might be impossible, though, with Cindee's eyes on the prize of the monarchy, being seen listening to someone whom she considered to be inferior was not a good look. Lee now thought he might, with some help from Liz, get Cindee to shut up and listen to reason, a tall order.

But it was Lee who had to listen. He stood there as Cindee continued venting her anger, repeating the same things before she started to walk away. She took a few steps and then stopped and once again began to list all the friends and close family members she lost because of Oscar and the failure of Queen V to defend what she called the borders of the colonies. This went on for several minutes as she recited each name out loud, including her relationship with each.

Lee turned and went back toward Liz, adrenalin pumping as he was eager to explain that he did not believe Cindee was on track, which scared him. Lee did not have to look far for Liz; he saw Reptan and Crocod standing in the distance and knew they would always walk with her. They kept up with her wherever she went, so Liz had to be close.

Lee had always considered them similar to enthusiastic rock star fan club members, who were always within arm's reach of the band leader. When Lee approached Liz, she again gave Lee a welcoming, compassionate hug, and an ear to listen to what he had to say about Cindee. She sat without comment throughout the one-way conversation and listened attentively to Lee.

At the end of his delivery, he paused, looking at Liz for a reaction. She displayed an expression to suggest she was neither pleased nor displeased, or even concerned, sad nor happy. All she gave him was a subdued diplomatic nod. Her reaction was to tell him that she was not sure how the other lizards, particularly Rex, would react to this. Liz thought Rex would either agree or disagree with it. She cared little about what action, if any, Rex would want to take, either with a group or on his own. She said that if given the chance, she would do her best to try to sit down with Rex for a calm, collective discussion about their next move as a team. Liz promised to, at least, get Rex and the other lizards to listen to all possible actions and hopefully and collectively come up with a response, one upon which everyone could agree by making it seem like it was their idea and in their best interest.

Reptan and Crocod still wanted to be on Liz's good side, so they were automatically on board. They listened and agreed with everything she said without interruption or facial expressions. Liz said she would take it to the other lizards, but this time with Rex in the audience. With Rex present, Liz calculated it would benefit the ants most if this guy were bitten.

"He could not get his medication fast enough," said Liz, holding up the prescription so everyone could read it. "In time, Oscar would be in grave danger, and with all of the heartaches that he has brought upon both ants and lizards, the ants would not be the only ones to benefit."

Liz explained that the ants would not be the only ones to be able to get to him and have him for food for a very long time. If something was to happen to him, she said, we should join them in this endeavor for a feast. Liz's change of heart resulted from following that old saying, "If you can't beat them, join them." She knew that Cindee would've unilaterally carried out this action, with or without her and the lizards, so she planned not to let the ants do it alone and instead to have them included, one way or another.

Liz's presentation was very convincing; she was joined at her side, as always, by Reptan and Crocod. After she was finished talking, everyone applauded, and eventually, all the other lizards joined in. This time, many ants, all within earshot, joined in.

Lee was silent, as was Cindee, who stood with her hands folded and a grin on her face, happy that it was not her job this time to convince the others that they should continue their pursuit, whether it be lizards or ants. They heard it all from Liz, whom she knew they all trusted.

With many ants and lizards now gathered around where the prescription was, this meeting was moved inside the opened bag. Cindee was happy that, in her mind, she was the one who managed to get all the ants to this spot. So, she began to speak to them in her usual fiery tone about wanting to go after Oscar and, of course, making an occasional jab at the queen, and she picked up where Liz had left off.

Lee and Liz stood side by side. Liz seemed to have gotten all the lizards onto her side, and to see her point of view, including Rex, she was surprisingly convincing that they should help the ants. They waited until Cindee finished what she had to say so that Lee could also say something, but only if he wanted to. Liz assured the other lizards that joining and standing by Lee was in their best interest. The other ants now agreed that attacking Oscar was best for both ants and lizards. She said that as Rex walked up towards her, put his hands around her shoulder, and patted her on her back.

Liz said this plan would ensure that no more gas, blowers, or water would ever again be used against them. And in the future, Rex continued, they should all learn to take matters into their own hands and defend themselves against those who seek to destroy them.

Cindee's talk with the ants continued for a while, which seemed like forever this time, and then it was Lee's turn. His voice crackled as he once again described the loss that had happened the days and times prior but without any mention of all the names and their relationships that Cindee had just gone over. Lee again talked about the loss from the very first significant feast, and he feared for the loss of the beloved queen and his family and friends. He spoke of how the current queen had gotten them through some of their life's roughest and most difficult times. He glanced at Cindee, who gave him two thumbs down when he praised the queen. He went on to say that although he felt that losing Oscar would place Oscar's family in the same situation as they had gone through, he now felt it would be justified for what Oscar had put them through. Oscar had one kid, his son Gene, and a wife who would be left behind in any attack. This kid and Oscar's wife, Penni, would be left without a father and a husband, but that is precisely what Oscar had done to them. Lee did his best this time not to appeal to their sensitive side.

Cindee was already convinced that most of the other ants would also, from now on, at least want to listen to her, thus raising her prospects at this time of becoming queen herself.

Some of the ants, albeit a tiny minority, were still afraid that the lizards would eat them, especially if they were to defy them and get in their path if they went against the collective plan. Lee and Cindee remained two of the only ants brave enough to cross the route of the lizards by not only going into their territory but also walking alongside, under, and around them. Perhaps by walking in such proximity to the lizards, Lee still hoped to convince the skeptical ants that the lizards were at least on their side for this project and the lizards had given their promise of rebuilding the mound. Lee assured the ants that they, the lizards, were not all bad. A small minority of the ants, though, still thought he and Cindee were crazy for being so trusting of the lizards.

Although he won the admiration of all the other ants, Lee still always found it most comfortable and safe when he stood in front of Liz, always by her front legs. He did this so the other small group of hesitant ants could see that at least Liz—even if the other lizards were not—was indeed friendly. Because of this, they could see that none of the lizards were attacking Lee. They saw how much the lizards stood and listened to his speech and how they nodded, signaling that they were willing to help. Even Cindee seemed to applaud him for his courage and speech, but she was discreet and showed her admiration and approval of him with a simple smile without saying a word.

This new evidence that Lee had found about Oscar's condition was a once-in-a-lifetime opportunity for everyone to avenge their family and friends, being that they, the ants, were not the only ones who now knew about it. Still, only they, the ants, could execute any plan effectively.

Cindee, however, thought they could use the help of other lizards, particularly Rex, should any unforeseen obstacle arise. Cindee was particularly concerned about any situation that could potentially change the minds of any lizard about their plan to attack Oscar. After all, only some of the lizards were present when the strategy was first discussed, so anyone who joined late might still need to be convinced. Liz may only be able to get to some of them in time to persuade them. To the other ants' and lizards' amazement, they were surprised to see how well they could work together, along with their newfound friendships, to put this particular plan in place. What they say is true, "The enemy of your enemy is your friend."

Speaking of newfound friends, no one seemed threatened by the arrival of a new friend, Crapo, who belonged to a species of frogs. Even the lizards accepted him, although he was more likely to eat lizards and unlikely to eat ants. He had always lived in Oscars' backyard and spent most of his time in one of the corners of the shed. Like all frogs, if Crapo's eyes blinked rapidly, he was eating. Looking into his eyes, one could tell, or at least presume, if he were hungry or full. Frogs do not have any teeth, and they are similar to serpents in that they have to swallow their prey whole, including any of the lizards. Whenever frogs are eating, and you look at their eyes, you will see their eyes sink to the back of the head; this happens because the eyes go to an opening of the skull so the food can pass through their throats.

Crapo was a bullfrog who met Liz long ago while growing up in Oscar's yard.

Very little was known of Crapo. Since Liz had never really mentioned him in any conversation, the little information that was available about him was, at the bare minimum, gossip. When Crapo first met Liz, though, he was wounded and could not walk. Seeing this, Liz was able to keep the ants from eating him at the time. From that day on, the two became friends, but lately, it had become more like a long-distance friendship. Crapo and Liz both knew that the ants, because of their vast numbers, could have easily overwhelmed him and eaten him to the bone, so he had always been Liz's friend, one that she knew she could always count on in times of trouble, and she needed the most powerful of friends to be at her side.

Liz and Lee were sitting together when she turned to Lee and asked, once the deal with Oscar was over, where would Lee like to build his new mound? Lee looked around and, after a brief pause, told her he did not want to return to the same place where they had the last two tragedies, as he feared a third time would be anything but a charm.

Liz said Oscar's son, Gene, would not get to attack them. "Once Oscar is gone, Penni or Oscar's son, Gene will not use gas on us," Liz said. "Besides, Gene is very lazy," she added. "He only likes dancing, watching cute animal videos on his phone, and playing video games. He would be hard-pressed to do any outside gardening or yard work anytime soon, *if ever,*" said Liz "Let us plan to relocate to a new location where ants, lizards, and frogs can live in peace and out of the path of Oscar or his remaining family. The end of the driveway, against a tree, would be perfect, or across the street in a different yard," Liz continued. "We can also be brave and build it directly under Oscar's front door as a direct warning or threat to Oscar that we are here to stay and regardless of what he does, he will never be able to get rid of us as too many memories inhabit this location, anyway," Liz continued. She then looked around and said, "Well, what about behind that rock?" and pointed to the rock where they hid from the blower the first time, they met Reptan and Crocod, just before they were about to fight. "We were able to withstand the hurricane winds the first time there. It is our lifesaver, our good luck charm, and it shielded us from harm in the past." Lee waited for a response. Reptan and Crocod walked over and joined Liz and Lee in the conversation.

Now, Reptan, Crocod, and ER have all joined. All three lizards listened to Liz as they looked over at the site and nodded to agree to this location behind the rock. Liz took the first step and began to walk over to the rock; Lee followed close behind. Liz turned her head and looked back, and she could see all the other lizards and Crapo joining on her trail—something ER must've done to alert or communicate with them about what was about to happen.

As they got to the rock, Cindee ran over and approached Crapo. And even though the two previously had not met, Cindee said, "I am here to join you, all of you, so let us all rebuild our home here." Cindee said she wanted to move the first set of dirt, and no one appeared to want to take that honor away from her. "We will need to determine where we will get the rest of the new sand to rebuild," said Cindee.

Crapo pointed and said, "Look, over there, under the leaves, at the end of the driveway. It is hidden from view, but there's a pile from which we can get all the dirt we need, and Oscar would never notice as it is covered with leaves."

Little did Crapo know that this was the dirt from the old mound that was blown away with the leaves and was now piled up in this location. Liz, Lee, and Cindee immediately recognized the area and the dirt. Still, except for Cindee, the others had yet to say anything.

"It would be great to rebuild using recycled materials from the old home in a new location," said Cindee.

"This would bring back memories," said Lee. "We would feel better knowing we had used so much of our past, so our friends and family memories did not go to waste."

One by one, the ants, led by Cindee, and then the lizards, led by Liz and her two lizard admirers and Crapo, walked over to the pile of leaves, and crawled under them. The leaf-cutter ants formed a line, and the fire ants carried the dirt while the leaf-cutter ants cleared away the leaves, with everyone having begun to move some of the sand. They left a clear path to go back and forth, as they always had, but this time with Cindee leading the way. She stood with her bullhorn and yelled as they passed, but unlike her previous rants, this was all motivation. While the lizards dug a hole, Crapo stood guarding as the sole lookout, and the ants started their march.

However, the ants' march usually follows a trail set by their pheromones. These pheromones are the chemicals released in the air, similar to perfume, which let all the other ants know where to follow and tell them where they've been. They communicate using the smell of this chemical, which is also excreted through their bodies. Using the antennas on their heads, they will stroke the antenna whenever passing by another ant. This brief encounter will help identify which colony the specific ants came from and dispatch various information, including food availability and its location.

As Liz and the lizards helped the ants rebuild their mound, Reptan and Crocod competed for Liz's attention. Although not as obvious this time, they competed to build different parts of the mound with the dirt at the end of Oscar's property. The construction went on, and everyone got involved. Whenever they got tired, they would pause and drink some water from Oscar's dripping water hose. They would also eat, and this was food that was blown away from the storage in the mound, plus food from Oscar's trash that was blown away during his cleaning which was now stuck there under all the leaves.

With most of the food particles now up against the tree, it was easy to scoop them up and transport them to the new mound. The success of salvaging whatever food they could fit into their holders, hands, and mouths depended on every ant working together. This was a monumental task but not a logistical nightmare. Taking food from the trash can and walking it back to the mound is a skill the ants have learned since birth. One of the only fears was that they might be seen should Oscar decide to leave his yard and spot them walking along, especially the leaf-cutter ants.

The mound rebuilding between the ants and lizards took over an hour. During this time, there were many new friends to be made along the way and many new alliances as well. Some fire ants took the time to get to know some leaf-cutter ants, and lizards did the same with other lizards. The ants and lizards learned things about each other that they never knew before just by working together. Their information exchange included the neighborhoods they came from, others they knew growing up, and those no longer around.

Oscar never came back outside to do any more yard work or to mess with the leaves, whether using a rake or the blower. He didn't return to take one of his trademark afternoon or early evening walks. Crapo was now joined by Reptan and Crocod and continued to stand guard as they feared that Oscar would return, perhaps this time with a trash bag or something to collect the leaves, which he has rarely done. Still, if he did, they feared Oscar would see the ants' trail and take further harsh action to eliminate them. But that fear was unfounded.

What was unknown to them then was that Oscar sometimes tended to leave the leaves there so they could decompose. He hoped they would once again become part of the soil under the tree; other times, he kept the leaves in a pile there for his grandkids to play in when they came over on selected weekend days. This way, the issue of leaves turned into a bonding moment he'd have with the grandkids.

With most ants going inside the mound to check out their new home, the lizards also started to disperse. The only lizards remaining were Liz, along with her two friends. Now that the construction of the mound was officially completed, Liz and the remaining lizards and Crapo, left as well. They said their goodbyes and farewells and hoped the goodbyes were meant only for right now.

Cindee joined Lee and called all the ants to get together for an impromptu meeting inside the new mound. At the same time, Reptan and Crocod volunteered to stand guard still outside. They continued to look out for Oscar or maybe other unfriendly lizards.

Inside the mound where this meeting was to be held were several place cards up and over the sides, including some posted on the walls of the mound as to who the candidates were for queen. Still, none of the signs suggested who you should vote for or why. The place cards stated who was aligned with whom and who would do what for whom if elected.

Despite all this information, no candidate was strong enough to challenge Cindee. This was the finding from the only debate that was held, and the polls that followed. None of the other candidates were able to match Cindee's campaign donations. The other two candidates were either minor or virtually unknown. Lee and some other observers thought two of the other candidates for queen were running to get their names out there, at least in preparation for the next election. Their goal in this campaign was not necessarily for the position of queen but for a lesser office position below the queen, which might also work to their advantage. After the elections, Cindee, probably the most well-known candidate, quickly garnered most of the vocal support, as the polls suggested, whether anyone else liked her or not.

To everyone's surprise, Cindee needed more votes despite the polls to win the royal position after the ants held their election later that week. As the last of the votes were tabulated, it turned out that the election was decided by about a few hundred or so ants who participated. One of the less popular ants was elected queen. She had one significant advantage: name recognition. She was Valerie, who was easily reelected.

Many remaining ants that came to the polls to vote required severe medical attention. Some appeared with broken legs and missing arms, and all lost at least one family member and or friend to the last tragedy, which now was causing them severe psychological problems. Since Cindee lost the election, the vote was seen by many as a protest vote, carried out by many of the men who did not like Cindee.

Even though Cindee lost the election, she vowed never to have the ants go through the devastation they had just gone through. Such a powerful campaign and commitment resonated with many of the ants, but it was not enough to give her the necessary victory. How she would accomplish this leadership role she vowed to carry out was never really clarified during her campaign concession speech. Most ants believed her, or at least thought she was the most capable of carrying out her promises and programs, albeit with a lot of help. Still, because she did not win, it was assumed that it was just her personality that people did not like. They lied to the pollsters that inflated her numbers.

Cindee did promise, however, during the campaign, that one of her priorities had she become queen would have been the appointment of a food and frug Commission czar who would now inspect every piece of food that came into the mound. This czar would have been set up to inspect and test primarily by sniffing every bit of the food for safety. She would have appointed Lee as the first member to head this new commission as he had the medical knowledge and first-hand experience to determine food safety. Cindee had also vowed to work with the lizards and strengthen their alliances to secure the mound and ensure it was safe and strong enough to withstand the destructive force of another attack. Cindee's campaign promises and priorities were noticed by many. It was widely believed that these promises kept her poll numbers so high. These promises did not go unnoticed by the newly reelected queen Valerie either, who thought perhaps this was what the people wanted.

As one of her first acts, the reelected Queen Valerie promised to address many of Cindee's promises, with particular attention to protecting and defending the borders of the colony and implementing her food safety program. The queen appointed Lee as her first knight for his bravery and knowledge of medications and antidotes that enabled them to fight certain illnesses. His diplomatic skills included ties of diplomacy and friendship, bringing the lizards and ants together, making friends with the likes of Crapo, and having the management skills to assemble all of them to help rebuild the new mound. Lastly, Lee gained recognition for being instrumental in the rescue from the last massacre, which made him a genuinely diplomatic leader, ideal for this unique and well-deserved position.

With the mound completed and the election over, Cindee appeared to be getting in touch with her softer side. She expressed this in a private conversation with Liz, telling her that she no longer distrusted Lee. She said she also had gained a newfound trust for the lizards, especially Liz. Cindee stated that she also had tremendous respect for Rex. One could only assume that the election loss had somehow humbled her.

Later that day, Queen Valerie sent out invitations to the lizards, Crapo, and all the ants to attend her inaugural ball. The purpose would be that everyone could get to know her better and congratulate her in one setting on her surprise victory, at least for those who wanted to do so. Everyone who got the queen's message accepted the invitation. Liz, Reptan, and Crocod also congratulated Lee on his new position, and they all pledged to drink and feast with each other until dark on the night of the ball.

That evening at the queen's ball, Crapo was a security guard at the entrance. Reptan and Crocod were standing close to each other when they saw Liz walking into the grand hall of the mound. She was beautiful. They noticed Liz had a new lizard accompanying her. They walked hand in hand and wore matching outfits. At first, the whispers were circulating, as no one knew who this new guy was who held her snugly as the two of them walked in. He was not a lizard they had met or seen before; neither ER nor Rex could identify him, and Lee was silent. He was young, handsome, and slightly taller than Liz, but he appeared equally athletic. He had a simple smile on his face as he walked towards everyone. Reptan and Crocod thought he was polite and, at the very least, certainly friendly. Everyone smiled back at him as he and Liz walked past them hand in hand. ER, Reptan, and Crocod were the most curious. ER was probably looking for information to spread some story, and although they were now friends, for Reptan and Crocod, seeing Liz with her new friend was something they had not expected, let alone accepted. Standing around and conversing with ER, they thought he was why she would not choose one of them, but they did not immediately inquire.

As the night went on, Reptan and Crocod eventually got up the nerve to say hi to Liz as she approached them while making her rounds in the ballroom, still holding this other lizard's hand. He still had a smile that seemed to be permanently painted on his face while he talked to other lizards, and Liz introduced him to them one by one. When it came time for Reptan and Crocod, standing next to ER, they got their answer. Liz introduced this new friend to them as her husband, Claus, who was stationed far away in the military for a long time. She explained that she met Claus in the army, as they were once on a ship together while they were both newly enlisted in the navy. Liz went on to say that the two of them dated for a while and got to know each other very well after spending free time with each other. After a brief courtship, they eventually married just before they were sent off to different parts of the globe. During this time, Liz had several years of military training, and she was the leader of their boot camp at one point. This is also where she learned her survival skills, how to build alliances and the value of saving a life and taking one if needed.

Claus' return home to Liz was an additional celebration, and all the ants at the ball received them together. Just then, a small crowd of even more lizards gathered around to hear his story, with particular interest in the part about how he met Liz. Excitement grew when he told them what he did in the military. Claus said, and Liz confirmed, that he was in the special forces, the equivalent of the Navy Seals. When asked by ER about any specific secret missions he was assigned, he placed his index finger over his mouth and said, "*Shhhh,*" with a wide smile. ER smiled back, and Eric said to Roger in a whisper, so he's a secret agent, man, and they both laughed. Claus walked away from Liz, who was still chatting with ER. Claus approached Lee, patting him on the shoulder.

Lee turned around, and they smiled, then Claus said, "Hello, my old friend, it's been a while since we last talked."

Lee nodded his head in agreement but did not say a word.

Claus then continued, "It is great to see Queen Valerie still on the throne; these colonies need a strong, brave woman to lead them, and none is more qualified than Valerie."

Lee turned his head to Claus and said, "Well, Valerie is just perfect for us, ants, for the lizards though, your wife, Liz, does an excellent job and is the perfect de facto leader, a job that only your long lost only cousin, Brandy could've done." Lee went on to say, "I remember the day Brandy died at the hands of Vergil; it was also the day I met your wife, Liz; she had an allure about her that made me not fear her on first encounter. We chatted, which I know comforted us both, and we have since become life-long friends. I have to say, I think you two are the luckiest people in the world to have each other."

Claus smiled back and said to Lee, "Brandy's passing at the hands of Vergil will never be forgotten. I know it has been impossible to get back at Vergil personally, but I will never forget, and cannot thank you enough, Lee, for organizing such a well-thought-out planned revenge on Vergil's owner, Mrs. Beck. I don't think I could've done it better if I did it myself," said Claus.

Lee smiled and said to Claus, "I'll do anything for an old friend like you, including being the best friend to your wife and making sure that none of the ants ever attack her."

Just then, Claus and Lee stopped talking as they turned to see Liz, who was still conversing with ER as she approached them.

In addition to Liz talking about his and her time in the military along with his service, she also mentioned some of his basic plans for the future, including building a new home for himself and Liz and possibly starting a family. The lizards stood there mesmerized by his tales, and ER were taking notes. They were very happy for him—at least—for Liz's sake, they all appeared so. Even Reptan and Crocod thought she deserved someone like this guy. Both Reptan and Crocod thought they could never measure up to Claus anyway, and deep down inside, perhaps each was happy the other one did not get to be with Liz.

After explaining her history with Claus to the other lizards, Liz said that she had seen enough death and destruction to last her a lifetime between serving in the military and the recent destruction of the ant mount. Doing so has inspired her not only to want to help save the lives of the ants but also to help rehabilitate their lives.

Although Liz seemed to contradict herself, she did say one of the only reasons she wanted to see Oscar hurt for his actions was so he could not repeatedly destroy their home. Taking her husband Claus by the hand and pulling him aside to speak privately, she told Claus she knew of Oscar's condition long ago. Liz said she knew this by reading one of his prescriptions once—something she never mentioned to Lee or any other lizards. Reptan, Crocod, and Lee walked up to listen in with Claus and join Liz's conversation, so Liz continued.

Liz said one day, a long time ago, she went into Oscar's house through a kitchen window that was always left open. She saw a prescription bottle lying on top of the counter when she walked in. Oscar's wife, Penni, came into the kitchen and saw her; Penni screamed, took off one of her shoes, and threw the shoe at Liz. Liz said the shoe barely missed her, but with Penni screaming, Oscar came running into the kitchen with what looked like either a rolled-up newspaper or magazine. Liz then ran and leaped off the countertop and sprinted out the window. Liz continued that she scarcely escaped, but she remembered seeing Oscar's meds on the counter, with an attached receipt that showed it was for an antihistamine medication. These medications came from a veteran's hospital.

While telling this to her husband, with Reptan, Crocod, and Lee all standing there, she instantly remembered that also she once read some of Oscar's trash and saw some of the other correspondence he would get in the mail from a foreign veteran's group. It caught her attention because it was not a regular veteran's group she had ever heard of. Many of their writings were not in English, but a part of the name had been ripped off. Liz paused, put one hand on her chin, and said, "hmmmm . . ."

Looking back, she said the only part of the name she saw was *Bundes*. Now, thinking back to her time when she was stationed in Germany, comparing it to what she discovered and what she had found in his trash, the rest of the word should've been, *wehr*. Yes, Oscar was part of the NAZI army. Since he had been out of the service, he continued to get correspondence from a foreign veteran's group, friends, and their sympathizers. This, Liz said out loud, made it so easy for Oscar to go out and hurt what he called "the vermin."

Holding Claus's hands, Liz said, knowing that the ants needed her help and being aware of what they had gone through at the hands of Oscar and what kind of person he was, she had to help. The wind picked up again a few minutes later, and it was getting darker. Surely Oscar would not come out at night to do more damage than he'd already done.

Laying on the steps in the backyard of Oscar's house, Blondi was enjoying a siesta. Above the steps, sitting on the windowsill, was Vergil, where he usually was in a position when he was about to bathe himself. A few of the red fire ants must've either been bored or had a scheme they now thought could come to fruition. Either way, seeing Vergil directly above Blondi gave them an idea that they soon spread among themselves. The fire ants' objective was twofold. Part one was to launch an attack on Vergil, followed by an attack on Blondie. They would have to be cautious, though, as these ants knew that any attack on Vergil would result in him licking the bite area, and they knew they would not survive when submerged for an extended period in Vergil's saliva. The ants were hoping they would leave a bad enough taste in Vergil's mouth, and that lousy taste the ants would leave in his mouth would mean he would have to spit them out. The ants thought that Vergil's spitting was something they could live with, as once Vergil spat them out, the ants could easily swim their way to safety, so they initiated their plan and attacked.

After the bite, every few seconds Vergil would give off a sneeze, one similar to when he had a hairball. Blondi initially appeared either unimpressed or not interested in anything Vergil did, especially during his nap time. The fire ants then approached Blondi, climbed up on his backside, and proceeded towards his ear. In a well-choreographed move, the fire ants launched their coordinated attack on the back of Blondi's ears. At first, Blondi used his sharp back paws and aggressively scratched his ear, but the fire ants anticipated this move. As soon as they bit Blondi, they ran toward the front of his face just above his eyes, where they knew he would not scratch. Just then, Vergil sneezed one more time; Blondi turned his whole body towards Vergil, thinking somehow Vergil's sneeze was the cause of his itch, perhaps an allergic reaction. After Vergil's third sneeze, Blondi raised his head slightly, looked up, and saw Vergil staring directly at him as if to say, "Yeah, I did that." Without giving Vergil a second thought, Blondi put his head back down, scratched once more, and resumed his siesta. The fire ants remained calm, thinking that their plan did not have the effect they had hoped, but just then, Vergil did sneeze again, but this time, Blondi did not raise his head; instead, just the one ear he was scratching and facing the direction of Vergil, who had now jumped down off the ledge and now was standing not too far from Blondi. Vergil ran down the steps and headed towards the front lawn.

Blondi came running across the front lawn chasing Vergil. The two ran so fast that they knocked over one of Oscar's trash cans. Blondi and Vergil stepped over the trash, and while running, Blondi tracked some debris raised by the wind, which flew toward where the ants and lizards were standing. One of the pieces of trash that came flying was a letter printed on noticeably thicker paper than the one used for the prescription, a paper similar to that of a postcard, but this was printed in English. ER got a hold of the letter and immediately read it out loud.

This letter was an invitation for a reunion of veterans who lost comrades in the last year, and the letter was addressed to Oscar from the same veteran's group for which he was in contact.

The letter stated, *We know that you have lost many more of your friends, and you are invited to a luncheon to honor those that have passed on in the last year.*

This gathering would be held at Eagle Nest Park, a local park located on the street next to Oscar's. Like many before, Oscar placed this letter in the trash. At first, some of the lizards thought that because it was placed in the garbage, it meant that perhaps Oscar did not want any reminders of those who had passed, or perhaps Oscar did not want anything to do with this particular group any longer.

Maybe he wanted to remember those who had passed as he had remembered them in his memories, and that's why the letter ended up in the trash. Reptan and Crocod said they thought this meant that Oscar indeed wanted to remember his fellow soldiers—the way he saw them when they were last alive.

Queen Valerie was among the ants that took particular interest as word got around about the picnic. She wanted to get the other ants from the different communities to attend this picnic at least, as it would be an excellent opportunity to gather food for storage since the park was over on the next street across from Oscar's house. Valerie wanted to get the message out that this was a function that the other ant colonies were to attend and get in on the food the veterans would be dropping. Valerie stated that all the food wrapped or unwrapped, eatable, and discarded was to be fair game.

Reptan, Crocod, and Liz made it a point to promise that they would not attend this function, as they thought it should be just the veterans and ants who should go to this picnic if they wanted. Reptan and Crocod said that even if Oscar did not attend, the veterans needed this time alone to be together and in peace, as they were not the ones who destroyed the mound.

It was getting late; the crowd was thinning, and everyone started to leave for home.

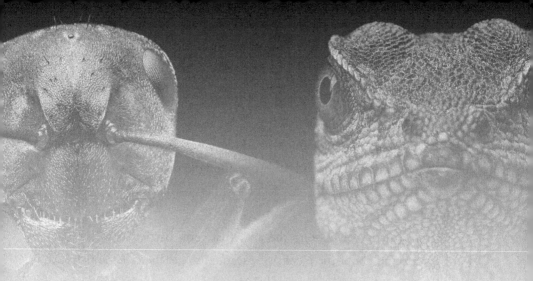

ays later, July 20th, was the picnic day. Oscar decided he would attend after all, and so did lots of the fire and leaf-cutter ants. Food was spread out everywhere, on tables and blankets alike. Lots of the food was also kicked around, adhering to the bottom of the shoes of some attendees sitting on the grass. This was good food; it was not only the stuff on the ground but also the food on the tables and the chair's armrests. As these men were in their later years, and so many needed assistance, dropping food was unavoidable.

The red fire ants from across the street smelled the food from far away, as did the lizards; even though some of the lizards did keep their promise not to attend the picnic, a few lizards, ER, Rex, and even Crapo heard, and were there primarily to make sure the food was safe. They also kept watch, ready to alert in case any of the other creatures might crawl up in the grass and disturb the ants with their feast.

As the picnic got underway, it was only a short while before it was time for the speeches. And to no one's surprise, the keynote speaker was Oscar. A round of applause greeted Oscar as he approached the podium. Oscar began his speech by talking about his time as a "guard for those in captivity" during WW2. He went on to talk about the friends and people he knew who went into the concentration camps to help with what he and his comrades called the "special operations." And yes, he did mention the vermin who went into these underground shelters. He said these were fellow citizens who were lost, including some of his extended family, without naming specific family members.

During Oscar's speech, there was a lot of cheering from many of the more than two dozen people in attendance. He continued by talking about how he managed to get out of the area and free from all the fighting, but as to how he made it to where he was today, that part was not included in his speech.

Oscar smiled as he went into details about going into this one particular room, where the people inside were all made to take off their clothes. He and his comrades would turn off the lights, wait silently, and then turn on the ice-cold water. He would laugh as he could hear the people screaming in fear, but it was just a shower. He laughed out loud at the irony as he told this to the audience, and everyone there understood, laughed, and applauded, many standing to do so.

After Oscar finished his speech, drawing a lengthy standing ovation, Oscar's son, Gene, walked up to the podium and began to speak. Gene talked about how, growing up, his dad always had nightmares. These nightmares were mostly about how they lost their home and everything inside the house. First, the Allied bombs, and then their second home lost to what he called the Red Army of thieves. Gene then went on to talk about how Oscar met his wife Penni, Gene's mom, a professional registered nurse at the time, and how, after the war, due to a mix-up and lousy directions, Oscar and Penni ended up on a train bound for Switzerland. They stayed in Switzerland for two years, finally got their passports, and immediately after, they made their way to America, where Gene was born. Gene did not specify what region of the country he was born in, but the mere fact that he was born in the US drew applause. Gene kept the rest of his speech short, basking in all the applause after the part about his birth in America.

He paused, tilted his head down, and slowly raised his head to face the audience, smiling. The crowd was silent.

Gene said, "I do remember one of the fondest memories I had with my father, it was when I first met Vergil, Mrs. Beck's cat. My father took two of my four pet lizards I had tied up with a string around his neck and accidentally fed them to Vergil, this turned out to be Vergil's first taste of lizard meat. From that day on, those vermin became a staple of Vergil's diet, the other two managed to escape." Gene said, sad look on his face, then he continued, "I would find these vermin, sometimes two or three at a time, and feed them to him. I guess you can say some fathers take their kids fishing, my father taught me 'Lizzing.'" Gene paused as he waited for the laughter and applause to subside, a laughter which he also could not contain.

After hearing Gene's story, the ants, Reptan, and Crocod, who were in attendance, were shocked, but just for Gene. Reptan and Crocod were shocked as these two, in particular, had never seen, heard, or encountered any time where Gene was mean to them. Hearing this now, tears ran down the faces of the lizards as they stood in silence; their heads bopped up and down, and their dewlaps kept extending and retracting. Although at first, they were angry that they did not go out to seek revenge on Oscar for what was done to them, now they just felt the same for his son.

As word got around to Rex and Cindee, Cindee was visibly shaking with anger. The same anger that Reptan and Crocod felt for Gene, now that all of those suppressed memories of being held captive when they were younger, came flashing back to the forefront. Cindee could not understand how this was missed.

She looked at them and asked ER, "How did you two not know about this guy? He seemed like he had a perfect childhood and bad parents," she said.

"How did we miss this, knowing what this guy has done to our friends and families?" said Rex, who was standing there with Liz's husband, Claus.

Rex told Claus that he was disappointed Liz did not tell them first what she'd found out about Oscar and his group, but standing next to Claus, he kept calm.

The speeches and attendees began to clear out as the picnic was winding down. The picnickers were emptying their plates in the trash, and as they did, even more food was dropping outside the now overflowing trash can. Cindee instructed the ants that this was the food they should take back to the mound, and Lee agreed. Word quickly spread to all the ants, including the fire ants, to join in the transport. All the ants joined forces and began their long march back to the mound. This process continued until the mound was so full of food that there was no additional food storage space.

Cindee, Liz, and Lee sat outside the mound at the end of the food gathering and congratulated each other on a job well done. Not only with the construction of the mound but also with gathering food. They knew now that all the ants could have enough food to last through the coming winter. If needed, the ants would share some of what they had gathered with the lizards. However, the lizards had their own stockpile.

They all felt better knowing that they were now friends. They saw in each other the things that had made them similar and not the things that made them different in such a way that they could want to mistrust each other. Perhaps it was knowing they all had a common enemy in Oscar. As the old saying goes, *the enemy of my enemy is my friend*. They all had suffered some extreme losses at the hands of Oscar, and in a strange twist of fate, even Oscar was now helping to keep them alive with all of this food.

At the end of the picnic and food-gathering, the newly recrowned Queen Valerie contacted ER. She had them send a queen's memo inviting all the lizards, ants, and Crapo to another inauguration feast at the new mound that was to be held that very same evening. She wanted to do this immediately, right now, as all the food that was left over from the picnic was too much to let go to waste. Even though she already had the inauguration ball, this would be another picnic to continue her inauguration festivities.

At about the same time, most of the crowd at the picnic had now disbursed. Valerie was grateful that there was now so much food in and around the mound that the lizards had to help by taking some food up into the trees for storage. A few ants even joined the lizards in transferring the food to the trees.

From up high in the trees, one could see both where the picnic was held at Eagles Next Park on one side of the neighborhood and their neighborhood on the other. The sounds of joyful laughter that could be heard coming from the trees of the ants and lizards were interrupted only by the whistling of the cool breeze whispering among the branches. Then, seemingly out of nowhere, all that fun was interrupted by the sound of an ambulance.

Everyone on the ground stopped what they were doing and ran up into the trees to see what was happening as the sound of the ambulance grew louder and then suddenly stopped. The lizards and ants looked over to where the sound was coming from. They saw that it was over where the picnic had just been held. By this time, many of the picnickers had already gone. The ambulance pulled up and three paramedics jumped out of the ambulance and approached the person lying on the grass. As the paramedics got close, they could see the condition of the patient who was in agony twisting his head side to side what most would consider to be abnormal behavior . A person lying on the ground, his limbs twitching around as if he was having a seizure. He was also bleeding through his nose as he was lying on his back on the grass, holding his left arm. It was Oscar, his son Gene, his wife Penni, and two of his buddies from his past who were at the picnic, one kneeled next to him. One of his buddies was standing over him, and the other kneeled next to him, trying to administer CPR. From up in the trees, there was silence as the lizards and ants looked on. With each press of his comrade's hand on Oscar's chest, bubbles of blood would come gushing out of Oscar's nose and now mouth.

Oscar's wife, Penni, was hysterical, screaming, "Oh my god!" and placing her now blood-stained hand over her mouth.

Her son Gene had his hands around her shoulders, trying to comfort her in her time of need, but they both appeared helpless. Gene held Oscar's hands, and they felt cold. Oscar's entire body was trembling, and his head moved side to side.

When the three paramedics arrived on the scene and rushed over to Oscar, one of them, without first asking any questions, immediately ripped off Oscar's shirt and continued performing CPR from where Oscar's friend was. The paramedics instantly noticed that this pattern of scratches, bruises, burn marks, and bleeding looked all too familiar, especially to these three paramedics. In particular, one of the paramedics commented that he had seen and had treated this type of situation in this very neighborhood before.

All over Oscar's skin they could see where he was scratching, where the red marks were, as he was now covered with red bumps, while his face and legs had begun swelling. The paramedics could also see all the food that was remaining and was scattered around from the picnic.

Following protocol, the paramedics asked Penni about any medication Oscar might be taking. Penni told them about the antihistamine medication that he occasionally took. Still, he didn't have any with him at the picnic today. Penni said, trembling as she was placing her hand on her forehead, that she seemed to have misplaced his prescription bottle, which she had sworn earlier that she saw the meds lying on top of the counter in the kitchen.

Not wanting to waste time, the paramedics picked Oscar up, placed him on the stretcher, and wheeled him into the ambulance. His wife and son accompanied him inside the ambulance, and they began to drive off. At the same time, the two veteran friends who were administering CPR followed the ambulance in their respective Buick and Lincoln. As Oscar's veteran friends drove off, the ambulance followed, tires screeching. The ambulance driver temporarily lost control of the steering wheel from a sharp turn on the misty grass and veered off the road slightly, hitting the curb so violently that it sent the front of the ambulance airborne. Just then, Vergil came running across the grass, chasing another lizard. Vergil was running so fast that the front of the ambulance, when it came down, struck Vergil in the head, knocking him out of the ambulance path and further onto the grass. When Vergil landed on his side, his white underneath had blood running down from his head and eyes. The lizard he was chasing stopped running, and turned around to see what had happened, but did not say anything. The ambulance continued on its way, the driver thinking the only thing he hit was the curb, so there was no need to stop. The lizard then walked towards Vergil, stopping just in front of Vergil's head, extended his dewlap, and licked the blood dripping from Vergil's head. It is said that hearing is the last of the five senses to go when someone dies.

The lizard then uttered, "Say hello to my friends when you meet them."

Vergil had reached his ninth life, and as the lizard turned to look in the direction of the others across the way up in the trees, he gave a thumbs up.

With the ambulance now gone, high up in the tree that was located next to the ants' new mound, Rex, Cindee, and some other fire ants could see the ambulance as it was driving away.

Queen Valerie came walking by the mound wearing a smile and holding a glass of wine. Several of her most loyal bodyguards were by her side, all wearing identical smiles. At this point, Liz's husband Claus was walking along with them, and then he climbed up the nearby dumpster with a long, narrow brown bag in his hand. He opened the brown paper bag and dumped the contents, a lot of small oval white pills, into the trash. After tossing the pills in the garbage, Claus climbed down and approached Valerie.

The queen walked over to meet Claus halfway and stood beside

Rex, Cindee, Lee, and Liz. As Claus approached Valerie and her loyal bodyguards, they raised a glass toward everyone. Claus smiled, and then the queen held up her orange tubular glass. Queen Valerie turned to face Claus and patted him on his shoulder.

Looking lovingly at him, she winked and said, "Thank you, here is a job well done."

Claus, standing next to Valerie's most loyal guards replied with his glass held high and said with a wink and smile, "Here's to another successful mission, from *Her Majesty's Secret Service.*"

Then Lee joined in, raising his glass as well, and facing Valerie, he said, "Here's to making the mounds great again and for queen and colony."

Printed in the United States
by Baker & Taylor Publisher Services